AMINATA COOTE

A Wife For Christmas

HopeLight Publishers

Love suffers long and is kind; love
does not envy; love does not parade
itself, is not puffed up; does not behave rudely, does not seek its own,
is not provoked, thinks no evil; does
not rejoice in iniquity, but rejoices in
the truth; bears all things, believes all
things, hopes all things, endures all
things.

1 Corinthians 13:4-7 NKJV

Contents

One

Chapter 1

Vivian Ebanks clenched and unclenched the fist in her lap, plastering on a fake smile as she addressed her employer's troubling statement.

"What do you mean I should take the week off?"

Her eyes drifted over the rows of bottles, their multi-colored liquids glimmering in the muted overhead lights, as she pondered his statement.

Cameron Grant chuckled, and she pursed her lips, glad he couldn't see her expression.

"I'm getting married in a week, Vivian. Thanks to you, I have an excellent wedding planner taking care of the details, so you don't have to."

Great. She was being punished for her efficiency.

"I'd be an asset to Robyn this week."

She'd been working with Robyn Fischer for the last six months to plan the destination weddings for the Porter twins and their fiances.

Although, to be honest, after the first few weeks, Robyn hadn't needed her help. She'd shadowed the woman to ensure she was doing a good job, and she was.

"This is not negotiable, Vivian." Cameron's voice was unwavering. "Weren't you the one who chastised me for not taking a break?"

"I didn't chastise you, exactly..." she trailed off as she remembered the embarrassing conversation.

It was a wonder her billionaire boss hadn't fired her. She probably had Mackenzie to thank.

Since Cameron began dating Mackenzie, he had become a new man. One who was insistent she take a vacation she didn't want. If she'd known his plan, she'd have remained in Portsville until the day before the wedding.

"Accept this as a Christmas gift from me and Mackenzie, and no logging on to do anything."

She gritted her teeth at the mention of Christmas. While she appreciated her Savior's birth, people's altered behavior during this season baffled her.

Until last year, she and Cameron had been in the same camp, treating it as just another day. She tried once more to get him to see reason.

"But sir—"

"No buts. Your temporary assistant is more than capable of covering in your absence. We plan to check with Robyn to verify that you're not hovering or offering to help her."

Vivian rolled her eyes as Cameron disconnected the call. What was she supposed to do for an entire week, surrounded by lovebirds with no work?

She drummed her fingers against the smooth wood of the bar

counter as she considered ways to occupy her time or sneakily defy Cameron.

It wasn't that she was anti-love. It was wonderful when people fell in love, but she didn't plan to be one of them. She was content to return to her apartment after work.

A picture of the neatly maintained space flashed in her mind, making her a liar. It was a place to sleep, nothing else. Perhaps she'd find a hobby.

A man in a business suit slid onto the stool beside her.

"I couldn't help overhearing your predicament." He leaned in too close for comfort, his malty breath heating her cheek. "I'd be happy to keep you company."

"No, thank you." She recoiled, holding her breath, not wanting to inhale the sickly sweet fumes emanating from him.

He winked at her, and her stomach churned with disgust. "We can loosen up together."

"No." She hardened her tone. "My boyfriend wouldn't like it."

"Where is he?" The man smirked like he knew she'd manufactured her male friend.

"He's coming." Her eyes wandered the room, seeking someone to rescue her.

Her gaze passed over most of the patrons, discarding them as too wrapped up in their issues to worry about hers.

Please, Lord. I don't want to be stuck with this man all night.

She could return to her room. But that supported Cameron's point she didn't have a life. He hadn't said those words, but her mind filled them in.

The man signaled the bartender. "We need beers." He held up three fingers. "One for me, my friend, and her imaginary boyfriend." He cackled, slapping his thighs as if he'd made the funniest joke in the world.

She scooted off the stool. Being a loser was better than hanging around with this drunk.

"Oh, don't go." The man grabbed her arm. "I was playing."

"Let me go, sir."

"No." His eyes narrowed. "When a man buys you a drink, you drink it."

"The lady said she wasn't interested."

Her knees wobbled with relief at Robert Porter Junior's familiar voice. His authoritative tone was as welcome as the man's foreboding presence.

Thank You, Lord.

Vivian shook herself free from the drunk man's suddenly limp fingers. She didn't blame him. Robert was an intimidating man.

"See," she slipped her trembling arm through Robert's, "I told you my boyfriend was coming."

Robert arched a brow but didn't refute her claim. She appreciated his willingness to step in as a temporary fake boyfriend, though the broody man was not her type…if she had one.

"Shall we go for dinner?" She smiled up at him, her eyes wide with pleading.

He nodded once. "Stay away from my girl."

Robert's growl was so convincing that the man slithered to his stool without another word.

"Sorry to keep you waiting." Robert placed a hand on her lower back. The heat of his palm sent a delicious awareness zipping through her. "Let's go somewhere else." He scowled over her shoulder and Vivian was grateful she wasn't the recipient of his glare.

Vivian followed Robert into the cool evening air. The perfection of his timing had her praising God.

Still, she dropped his hand when they were away from the building. His nearness affected her in a way she didn't want to investigate.

"Care to explain what that was about?"

A sharp gust of air rippled over her exposed skin, making her shiver as she wrapped her arms around herself. She should have brought a sweater.

"I wasn't in the mood for company."

"So you invented a boyfriend?"

When he said it like that, she felt like an idiot. She angled her chin.

"It seemed like a good idea at the time."

Robert snorted. "If you don't want to be picked on, maybe you shouldn't dress like a…" he gestured to her outfit. "What are you wearing?"

Vivian glanced down at herself. Her mint green pantsuit was as immaculate as it had been when she'd dressed earlier, thinking of getting some work done while she had dinner.

"There's nothing wrong with my clothes."

She was fastidious, aware that sometimes you only got one impression. Once people made a snap judgment about you, it was hard to change their minds.

"I thought personal assistants wore practical clothes, making it easy for them to blend into the background?"

She narrowed her eyes at him. He disapproved of her outfit because it was stylish? Unbelievable.

"And I thought soldiers had manners, or at least treated women with respect?" She straightened her jacket, though there was nothing wrong with it. "Don't worry. I'll stay out of your way."

She spun on her heels and stalked away. Insufferable man.

Two

Chapter 2

RJ Porter stared after Vivian's disappearing form. He had to admit that it was an impressive sight. The woman had curves for days.

He'd taken one look at her earlier and found himself fantasizing about a future with her. Foolish. Despite his mother's claim, people didn't fall in love at first sight.

Love meant getting to know someone and both people choosing to work on their relationship. He gritted his teeth. Not that she'd give him a chance after what he'd said.

He had sisters. He knew better than to imply a woman deserved the negative attention some men bequeathed like it was a gift.

"Vivian." He hurried after her, his pace slower than usual. He winced as the exertion irritated his healing wound. He pressed a hand against the spot, hoping to ease the tension. "Can you please wait?"

He stepped in front of her, forcing her to stop.

"Why? So you can tell me that global warming is my fault?"

His lips twitched at her sassy response. "I'm sorry. I shouldn't have intimated that what happened inside was your fault."

He'd gone a little crazy when he spotted her cozying up to the man at the bar. Jealousy had tightened his chest, and he almost walked away. It had taken a second to register that Vivian wasn't happy with the man's attention.

It was shocking to encounter that kind of behavior at this exclusive villa. But he supposed people were people wherever they were, regardless of their wealth.

"Let me make it up to you."

She stared at his midsection. "What's wrong with your stomach?"

"Nothing." He dropped his hand, trying not to flinch. "Let me take you to dinner."

He was practically begging her to eat with him. Anything was better than returning to the villa with his family.

Cameron and Xavier, his sisters' fiances, had rented three villas at the exclusive Cerulean Hideaway Resort in Greenvale. The bridal party and their families were staying for the week leading up to the wedding.

It was a beautiful space—a home away from home. The problem was it brought all the troubles of home, including his tense relationship with his father.

His father couldn't understand why RJ wasn't overjoyed to continue the tradition of breathing life into old furniture and family heirlooms.

"Will you take me somewhere nice?"

Her teasing smile gave him hope.

"Well," he lowered his voice to a pseudo-whisper, "I hear

there's an excellent restaurant nearby."

Whoever had put the welcome packages together had included a map of the resort, including its amenities. There was also a local map and a list of attractions, but that was an adventure for another day.

He planned to spend as much time away from the villa—and Robert Porter Senior—as possible.

"What do you say?"

She rolled her eyes. "You know everything was paid for upfront, right?"

He wagged his eyebrows. "Then we should splurge and eat whatever we want."

She gnawed on the corner of her bottom lip, her expression uncertain. His stomach clenched as he waited for her response, surprised by how much he wanted her to say yes.

"Alright." She threw up her hands. "I don't want to go to my room, anyway. Lead the way."

He tucked his hands into his pockets and headed for the nearest restaurant. He said nothing for the short walk, enjoying the cool evening breeze.

The air bore a hint of salt, and RJ itched to go snorkeling. He suppressed the urge, as it would be several more weeks before that was advisable.

As they entered the restaurant, soft candlelight flickered on the walls casting a warm glow. The murmur of conversations and the clinking of cutlery created an intimate atmosphere.

This was the perfect place to take a date. He glanced at Vivian, wondering if she'd get the wrong impression. A server approached them before he could suggest they try a different restaurant.

The slender man showed them to their table, where RJ pulled

out Vivian's chair and seated her. She arched a brow at him as he sat across from her.

"As you said, I know better." Shame curled in his gut. "Again, I apologize."

She waved away his apology. "I've already forgiven you. Let's move on."

She opened the menu and placed an order. He quickly did the same.

"Why don't you want to return to your room, Robert?"

He grimaced. "It's RJ." The desire to come clean with this woman he'd just met was so strong, it caught him by surprise. He settled for a half-truth instead of baring his soul. "Too many people."

She studied him. "Aren't you used to that?"

"Doesn't mean I'm always in the mood for it."

Sometimes he needed to be outside, away from the pressing needs and expectations of everyone.

"Shouldn't you be ecstatic to spend the week at the Nutcracker?" He feigned an expression of supreme enjoyment.

Someone had nicknamed the villas Candy Cane Castle, Nutcracker Palace, and Reindeer Hall.

"Who came up with those names, anyway?"

A grin teased the corner of her mouth, drawing his attention, and for a second, RJ forgot what they were talking about.

"I believe it was your niece."

"Excuse me?" RJ blinked, refocusing on her eyes.

"Gracie named the villas."

He pressed his lips together. "Of course she did."

Alana Grace was Madison and Xavier's daughter.

"You're lucky Xavier and Madison talked her down. She wanted us to decorate each villa to match the name."

RJ mock-shuddered. "I'm glad she didn't win that battle."

Living in a space decorated with giant tin soldiers and their menacing smiles would not be fun.

"Why are you avoiding the villa?"

Vivian dropped her gaze. "I'm on an enforced vacation."

She said the words like they were a curse. He cocked his head.

"Isn't that a good thing?"

"No." She glared at him. "What will I do for seven days if I can't work?"

"Ah."

He understood her struggle well. After his last mission ended with him receiving a stab wound in the gut, he'd been on sick leave. Once the doctor discharged him from the hospital, he realized how interminable the time was when you couldn't fill it with constant activity.

"What do you normally do on your days off?"

"Work." She said the word, barely moving her lips.

"That's it?"

"No." She hunched her shoulders. "I go to church. Exercise. Clean my house. Do chores."

"What about hobbies?"

She glared at him. "Why am I the only person at this table exposing their secrets?"

He raised an eyebrow at her sharp tone. "I didn't realize the questions would bother you."

He glanced around the restaurant, searching for a subject that wouldn't offend her.

This week would become more uncomfortable if he irritated the one person outside his family with whom he'd had an actual conversation.

Their server took that moment to show up with their meals and RJ exhaled, the tension leaving his shoulders.

The spices wafting from his pot roast and mashed potatoes made his mouth water. Her roasted fish with vegetables smelled delicious, too.

"I'm sorry," he said after the server left.

He'd apologized more to this woman in the short time he'd known her than to people he'd known for years.

It was time for a change of topic. "Do you know why they have us here a week early?"

He figured she'd have more details since she was Cameron's assistant. Although, if he didn't spend so much time away from his family on missions he couldn't talk about, maybe he'd also be aware of the plan.

"It's a bonding experience."

"Bonding?" He cut into his roast beef, intrigued and horrified by the idea. "Why?"

"Marriage is hard enough when you're blending two families. Your sisters are merging three—four if you count Ella and her family."

He was still wrapping his mind around that. Before he'd left on his last mission, his sisters were single. When he returned, they were engaged, and he had a five-year-old niece.

He wasn't sure he'd gotten the full story and needed to sit down with his sister Madison to probe for details.

"What are their plans?"

Vivian leaned across the table. "If I told you, Soldier Boy, I'd have to kill you."

Three

Chapter 3

He couldn't sleep. RJ opened his door a sliver, listening for activity. At the silence, he left his room and padded down the hall, his whittling kit in hand.

After their initial squabbles, he'd enjoyed his dinner with Vivian, but it had stirred his longing for a family. He thought he'd buried that desire.

Pale moonlight filtered through the glass doors, casting soft, silver beams on the tiled floor. They illuminated the space enough, so he didn't need to turn on a light. He was glad.

So far, he'd stayed out of his father's way. But it was a double-edged sword. He'd escaped the conflict but had hardly seen his mother or sisters.

He grabbed a dustbin, opened the door, and sat on one of the lounge chairs near the pool. The distant hum of crickets and the faint ripple of the wind on the water created a soothing symphony.

RJ soaked it in before pulling out a knife and the small carving he was working on. The smooth wood grew warm in his hands as he shaved off delicate curls, the knife's blade whispering against the grain.

The activity kept his hands busy while his mind wrestled with the problem. This was day one, and he had six more to survive.

He rubbed his forehead. "Maybe I shouldn't have come."

"Why not?"

He started at Vivian's voice. He hadn't noticed her sitting in a chair shielded by the shadows.

"What are you doing here?"

A groan threatened to escape but he bit it back. Vivian made him forget to guard his words. Sadly, that meant he usually sounded harsher than he intended.

"I couldn't sleep. I hoped sitting in silence would bore me enough so I'd become drowsy."

"I can help you with that." RJ packed away his carving and tools.

"What's that?" Vivian pointed to the kit.

"Nothing." He grabbed the bin and headed for the villa. "Coming?"

"You know I am." She met him at the door and peered into the bin. "Why does your 'nothing' leave wood shavings behind?"

He sighed. "Has anyone ever told you that you ask too many questions?"

An emotion he couldn't identify flashed across her face. "No. Has anyone told you that you have too many secrets?"

He nodded to concede the point. The woman didn't let him get away with anything. He sensed that he'd never tire of sparring with her.

"Where are we going?"

"To the kitchen." He hurried ahead of her and dumped the shavings into the large bin. Hopefully, by the time his family awoke, the staff would have emptied the trash.

He flicked on the switch, confident the light wouldn't disturb anyone upstairs, forcing them to investigate.

"Sit." He gestured to the cushioned white chairs around the marble counter closest to the silver range. "When my sisters were younger, they had trouble sleeping."

He rummaged through the cupboards, removing a saucepan. He added two cups of milk and set it on the stove to warm.

"We found that hot chocolate and a few minutes of conversation did the trick." He threw a dish towel over his shoulder and leaned on the counter. "Pretend I'm an unknown bartender. What's troubling you tonight?"

She stared at a spot beyond his shoulder, her brows furrowed. "I don't belong here."

Her shoulders slumped. Gone was the effervescent and sassy woman from earlier that evening. Loneliness emanated from her every pore.

"Why do you say that?" He squirted a generous amount of chocolate syrup into two mugs and poured in the warm milk.

"Isn't it obvious?"

"Not to me." He handed her a spoon and a cup. "Stirring is part of the magic."

He remained on his side of the counter where he could see her face.

"I'm the assistant. I shouldn't be at the villa with the brides' family."

He tilted his head. "Where should you be instead?"

"I don't know," she mumbled, bringing the cup to her mouth.

"Staying with the rest of the help."

Compassion squeezed his heart. She felt insignificant, an emotion he had experienced more often than he cared to admit.

Lord, Vivian feels insignificant, as if she doesn't matter. Please give me the right words to encourage her.

"Nobody here sees you as the help."

She snorted. "How do you know? Have you met Irene Grant?"

He frowned, unable to connect a face with the name.

"Cameron's mother," she clarified. "Mrs. Grant would not be happy that I'm staying in the same facilities as the wedding guests."

"Is she here?"

He didn't remember the woman, but Vivian had transfixed him during the introductions.

"No."

"When is she coming?"

Vivian shrugged.

"So," he drew the word out. "You're worried about the opinion of someone who isn't at the villa?"

"She has a room here because we don't know when she'll show."

"Uh-huh." He nodded. "This is my opinion. Irene Grant isn't here." He held up a hand when she opened her mouth to argue. "We don't know when she'll show up or what she'll say about you. Don't waste time worrying about something that may not happen."

"If you knew how horrible she was, you wouldn't be so casual."

Her pout made him want to kiss her.

"Vee," the nickname slipped off his tongue. "You knew this

before you came. Sure, you thought you'd be working, but you had all the facts. You could have remained in Portsville until the wedding. You didn't. Secretly, you wanted to be part of this week's events."

She jerked as if he'd slapped her.

"I'm sorry." He raised both hands. "I didn't mean to offend you."

He stared beyond her as he contemplated his next words.

"Sometimes, God puts us where we need to be, though we would rather be someplace else."

His words resounded in his spirit. Is that what was happening? Had his injury and sisters' weddings been part of God's perfect timing?

She smiled ruefully. "You always seem to say the thing I least want to hear, but what's necessary." She sipped her hot chocolate, her eyes meeting his over the cup's rim. "Why didn't you want to be here?"

He grimaced. "We're mirroring each other's emotions today."

"Hmm, and you're excellent at diversion."

She was sharp. He decided to answer her.

"My sisters are getting married, and instead of being happy to celebrate with them, I'm wondering when the confrontation with my dad will happen."

"You're expecting a confrontation?"

His left eye began throbbing. "There's always one."

RJ and Robert Senior had argued about the same thing for most of his life.

"I'm sorry the relationship with your father is strained. But instead of waiting for an argument, find him and work things out before it ruins your sisters' weddings." She brought her cup to the sink. "Thanks for the hot chocolate, RJ."

"Anytime."

"Night." She paused on the threshold. "I suspect your sisters' insomnia had more to do with spending time with their big brother than an inability to sleep. You're a good listener. I hope you follow your excellent advice."

Four

Chapter 4

A knock startled Vivian from sleep.

"Yes?"

She cleared her throat as she glanced at the clock—she'd overslept.

"Coming." She hopped out of bed and strode across the plush carpet to open the door.

"You're not dressed." Mackenzie Porter took in Vivian's plaid pajamas, brows raised in surprise.

Mackenzie herself was impeccable in an ankle-length black and white sundress.

"Sorry. I'm running behind schedule." Vivian stepped back to let Mackenzie into her room. "I got in late last night."

"I know." A sly smile crept over Mackenzie's face. "You and my brother, huh?"

Vivian jerked. "It's not like that. I was at the bar and he rescued me from this guy who was coming on too strong." She was babbling but couldn't stop herself. "We had dinner and then we walked…"

She broke off at Mackenzie's amused expression.

"Anyway," Vivian laughed nervously. "That's all it was. Nothing for you to worry about."

Or to report to Cameron. Could she lose her job for having dinner with her boss's future brother-in-law?

"Pity." Mackenzie flicked the hair off her shoulder. "RJ could use a woman to mellow him out. Anyway," Mackenzie pointed at Vivian. "Is that what you're wearing? You're on vacation, but that's too casual."

"Can't I sit this one out?"

The last thing she wanted was to spend her day traipsing all over the resort.

What else are you going to do?

She ignored the niggling thought.

"This week is for your family." She smiled, hoping to convince Mackenzie to leave her behind.

"No." Mackenzie was adamant. "Cameron and I want you to enjoy this week as well. You've been a wonderful assistant, and we want to show our appreciation."

Mackenzie's words touched her. Technically, Vivian was Cameron's assistant, but it was nice of Mackenzie to acknowledge her role in his life without seeing her as a threat. It boded well for their future relationship.

"I'll get dressed."

"Excellent." Mackenzie beamed at her. "I'll wait for you outside…in case you're considering sneaking away or locking yourself in your room."

Vivian rolled her eyes, amazed at how well the woman had figured out her intention. She stalked to the closet and grabbed the first outfit her hands landed on. "I'll be out soon."

Mackenzie nodded with approval when Vivian met her in the hall. "I love that color on you."

"Thanks." Vivian smoothed a hand over the plum jumpsuit. Would RJ like this color on her?

She banished the unwelcome thought. Just because they'd had dinner and a few conversations didn't mean she cared what he thought about her fashion choices.

"Where are we going?"

"Downstairs." Mackenzie frowned at Vivian's shoes. "You may want to change your shoes."

She glanced down at her black wedges. "They're comfy." And were perfect with her outfit.

Mackenzie shrugged. "Alright."

Vivian ran her hand along the gold railing as she descended, surveying the group gathered on the plush white couches in the spacious living room. A giant pine stood naked in one corner. As Christmas trees went, it was lackluster.

Even so, it added to the ambiance, its piney fragrance mingling with lemongrass tea and the buttery smell of fresh croissants.

"Grab a seat," Mackenzie encouraged with a wave. "We'll be here awhile."

Vivian scanned the room, gaze flicking past the lush, strategically placed plants, searching for the best place to hide without earning Mackenzie's ire.

Vivian grabbed a croissant, which she nibbled on while lurking at the edge of the group. The wood-paneled column was the perfect shield.

The couples took center stage, attracting everyone's attention. They were gorgeous and well-suited. Xavier Washington's love for Madison was as obvious as Cameron and Mackenzie's affection.

Would she ever find someone who looked at her the way these men stared at their brides? Her stomach clenched, the familiar pang of self-doubt gnawing at her.

Who's going to fall in love with a chubby, untidy girl?

Her mother's unkind voice was so loud in her mind that Vivian flinched.

Love wasn't for women like her. She would remain single for the rest of her life, and that's the way she liked it.

The familiar reassurance didn't bring her the comfort it usually did, but she blamed it on the environment. Once she got away from the lovebirds, her emotions would readjust.

"Thanks for joining us." Xavier addressed the group. "We've dubbed the Nutcracker "Wedding Hub" as it's the central villa—"

"And because the princesses are here," Madison interrupted.

"I want to be a princess." Avery folded her arms and pouted.

"Me too," Gracie responded, mimicking Avery's posture.

The girls were the same age and had become fast friends.

"Tell you what," Levi Armstrong, Avery's uncle and Cameron's best man, knelt beside the girls. "When you grow up and get married, you'll be the princesses and everything will be all about you."

Both girls beamed at him.

"Promise?" Avery held out her pinkie.

"Promise." Levi hooked her pinkie with his, sealing the deal.

"As Xavier said," Cameron continued. "Nutcracker is the hub, so we'll have meetings and most of our activities here."

"Now," Xavier clapped his hands. "Who's ready to have some fun?"

"Me!" Gracie jumped up, pumping her fist into the air.

Gracie's enthusiasm elicited chuckles but created a pang of longing in Vivian's heart. Why hadn't she considered that singleness meant no children?

Vivian distracted herself by studying the occupants of the room. The air was festive and relaxed as everyone, except herself, was excited about the upcoming events.

Her eyes drifted to RJ, who leaned one shoulder against a wall on the opposite side of the room from his parents. A muscle in his jaw flexed.

Vivian glanced at the Porters. Robert Porter Senior glared at his son while Margaret's gaze flitted between her husband and son.

This was the tension RJ had referenced. She'd monitor the Porters so their drama didn't spill out and ruin the twins' wedding.

The tautness in her shoulders eased at the thought of being productive this week. She'd earn the twins' gratitude and maybe even a bonus if she ensured they had a wonderful wedding.

"RJ, Vivian, and Jacqui." Mackenzie's announcement brought Vivian out of her thoughts.

"What?" She glanced around, trying to piece together what she'd missed.

Cynthia Williams raised a hand.

"Yes, Cynthia?" Xavier acknowledged his former mother-in-law.

"Jacqui's not here. She left early this morning."

"Will she be back soon?" Madison queried in a soft voice.

"I don't think so," Cynthia admitted. "She brought her art supplies."

"Oh, well," Mackenzie shrugged, "I guess that means RJ and Vivian's team are short one member."

Madison waved a hand. "They'll be fine. This will even out the chances for everyone else."

A grin crept over Mackenzie's face. "Perhaps a new alliance will be forged today."

Vivian frowned. What was Mackenzie up to? And why did she have a sinking feeling that whatever Mackenzie was scheming involved her?

After the meeting RJ weaved across the room toward her, carrying a small bag with the villa's logo. The rest of the group dispersed as they collected their packets and found their team members.

Vivian braced herself, uncertain which version of himself he'd present today.

Would he be the chivalrous gentleman, the jerk, or the companion who'd entertained her?

"Hello." She nodded, using a napkin to wipe the crumbs from her fingers.

"Hi. We're working together."

"On what?" She'd helped plan the events, but didn't know what order they'd be in. She hadn't read the welcome package as she'd planned to work and didn't think the activities applied to her.

RJ arched a brow. "Wedding Puzzle."

She cocked her head. That had not been on her list.

"What's that?"

"Weren't you the one who had all the answers yesterday?" He dangled the bag over her head.

"Yesterday," she spoke through gritted teeth, "I wasn't supposed to be a participant."

She had fully expected to exclude herself, assuming Cameron would be fine with her decision as long as she didn't work. She should have known better. Her boss was a fan of shaking up the status quo.

"Do you mind if I eat breakfast?" One croissant wasn't enough fuel for her.

"You'll have to carry it with you." RJ pointed to a sheet of paper. "According to the rules, we must leave in five minutes or lose fifty points."

She arched a brow. "What's the prize?"

RJ shook his head. "It doesn't say." His eyes met hers. "But does it matter?" He leaned in, lowering his voice. "Are we letting these people beat us?"

She scanned the wedding guests. The thrill of a competition made her heart race. "No, we're not."

She darted to the buffet, grabbing a starfruit, two guavas, and another croissant. She ran outside with RJ with two minutes to spare.

"Where are we off to?"

He clicked a key fob, gesturing to the vehicle whose lights flickered. "That's us." He opened the door for us. "Your chariot, Queen of Curves."

"Why are you calling me that?"

"Aren't we doing nicknames?"

She frowned. "I don't know what you're talking about."

"You called me Soldier Boy. I've nicknamed you Queen of Curves." He winked. "QC for short."

She rolled her eyes, ignoring how her heart pounded at his private nickname for her.

"Let's go, QC, we have a game to win."

Vivian studied him out of the corner of her eyes as she

buckled her seatbelt. In another life, they may have been friends. She shook away the thought.

"You haven't told me what we're doing." She bit into her guava.

"Each team has a picture of the couple to assemble. We have GPS coordinates for the locations of the various puzzle pieces." He concentrated on driving. "The first team to collect the pieces and assemble their puzzle wins."

"That doesn't sound hard." She bit into the croissant, moaning as the buttery pastry melted on her tongue. "We'll split the list. Divide and conquer."

"We can't separate. The aim of this game is teamwork. If we're more than ten feet apart before all the teams return, we lose."

Five

Chapter 5

RJ tightened his grip on the steering wheel as he pretended to ignore Vivian. An impossible task as her fragrance had drifted and filled the interior of the SUV until every breath he inhaled was of roses.

He parked in front of a botanical garden. "We're encouraged to take pictures." He handed Vivian one of the disposable cameras.

"You're kidding? Don't you think that's going overboard?"

"Have you met my sisters? Smile." He pointed the camera and snapped a photo of her. "Just be glad this wedding isn't taking place in Cinnamon Hill. Otherwise, they'd have spies checking on us to ensure we follow their rules."

It wouldn't surprise him if the twins planned to review the photos to confirm they hadn't broken the ten-foot-apart rule before awarding a winner.

"Okay." She studied the photo they'd be piecing together. "I hope they gave us giant puzzle pieces."

"We have coordinates for four locations."

"Great." Her face lit up. "We should be done within the hour."

He suspected that wouldn't be the case, but didn't want to shatter her excitement.

Vivian drew in a breath and thrust her shoulders back. "What's the first clue?"

RJ forced himself to look at the paper, trying to focus on the clue instead of the captivating woman beside him.

"Make a wish, but don't take a sip."

"Make a wish, but don't take a sip." She mulled over the words, spinning in a slow circle. "What do people wish on?"

"Stars. Wishbone. Pennies."

She stopped, eyes widening. "Wishing well. Do you think the garden has one?"

He shrugged. "Let's find out."

RJ strolled through the wrought-iron gate of the botanical garden and walked into paradise.

Lush greenery, in an array of rainbow colors, spread out below them. In the center, stood a large fountain.

Vivian gasped. "It's beautiful."

"It is." The air was thick with the fragrance of jasmine and honeysuckle.

He snapped a few pictures, knowing they wouldn't come close to capturing the beauty. "Come on."

He led the way down the stairs. At the bottom, Vivian joined him and they followed the cobblestone path.

"Can you imagine how beautiful the Garden of Eden was?"

Birds chirped in the distance, combining with the soft rustle of leaves to create a peaceful symphony.

"I can't," he admitted. "My imagination's not that good."

The splendor was magnificent, but it was difficult to visualize a place without sin or blemish.

"I'm determined to make it into the kingdom and live on the new Earth." She glanced at him. "Aren't you?"

RJ focused on the path ahead. He'd grown up believing in God and accepted Jesus when he was ten. But that had been a long time ago. Before he became a soldier and did things the average person never thought of.

Could he make it into the kingdom after everything he'd done?

He lengthened his stride, ignoring the twinge in his stomach as the accelerated pace agitated his wound.

"So I take it you're not a Christian?"

RJ glanced down at the woman, who was once again in step with him.

"I am a Christian, just—" he slowed so she could walk and talk without gasping for breath.

"What?"

He stopped in front of the fountain and studied her.

"At what point does a person's sin become insurmountable? When do we get beyond salvation?"

She brushed his hand, the warmth of her touch grounding him in the present. "Is this because of what you've done in the army?"

He gave a single nod.

"I understand. Not what it means to be a soldier, because I've never served." She swallowed, her throat bobbing. "I understand how it feels to believe you're undeserving of grace."

What scars was this beautiful woman hiding to make her feel undeserving of God's love?

"That's the thing about grace, RJ. None of us deserve it, yet

God bestows it on us, anyway.

"And before you internalize the lie that your sins are too scarlet, Soldier Boy, remember David. He killed lots of people yet God called him a man after His own heart.

"It's not about what you've done or the sins you've committed, it's how you relate to God after the fact.

"Do you turn away from God or run toward Him? That's what determines a man's character—whether he can recognize his foibles and go into the presence of His Creator. His ability to accept the grace waiting for him there."

She snatched the laminated photo piece from the underside of the fountain while her words detonated in his heart like missiles.

He was silent on the trip to the car. Was she right? Had he turned his back on God because he feared being rejected?

A reminder of the fights he'd had with his father flashed through his mind.

Robert Senior couldn't understand why taking over the antique business wasn't RJ's dream. Since the business had been in the family for three generations, Robert saw it as a sign that it was meant to be forever.

His dad interpreted RJ's desire to forge his own path as a betrayal. It made for some interesting family dinners over the years, and almost always resulted in his mom calling a ceasefire. His relationship with Robert Senior became so strained that RJ rarely went home.

Had he expected God to be disappointed in him because his earthly father was?

Six

Chapter 6

Vivian feigned interest in the scenery while RJ drove to the next location. The robotic voice of the GPS and the hum of the engine served as a backdrop for her whirring thoughts.

What right did she have to tell this practical stranger how to live his life? Besides, she was a hypocrite…lecturing him about grace when half the time she struggled to accept it.

The psalmist was right. What is man that God should care for them? They were fickle in hearts and minds.

"I'm sorry."

He'd apologized to her so many times, the least she could do was admit when she was wrong.

He glanced at her before shifting his attention to the road.

"For what?"

"I shouldn't have attacked you at the gardens. I know nothing about you and shouldn't have made assumptions."

"You were right. I don't live as if God's grace is sufficient to cover my sins."

His lips curved into a rueful smile. "I've spent years dwelling on the fact that I've done things I'm not proud of. I should have taken my failings to God whose strength is made perfect in my weakness.

"I know some Bible." He smirked. "I'm not a complete heathen."

"It's not about quoting Scripture—the devil does that. It's about our ability to live out the truth of God's Word in our daily lives."

What was wrong with her? Her mouth had gone on autopilot and was running ahead of her brain.

"Right again. You've snuck into my brain and read my secret thoughts."

No, but she'd stared into a mirror for years and blasted him with every revelation she'd received. How should she handle the realization that the things she'd struggled with for years also affected him?

"We're here." RJ parked beside a bus and shut off the engine.

Vivian squinted at the colorful sign. Whimsical World Amusement Park. "You've got to be kidding."

Her breathing became shallow at the thought of entering. She forced herself to take calming breaths.

RJ chuckled. "Nope. The Porter Pranksters have struck again. I hope your shoes are comfortable. We may be here for a while."

Vivian glanced down at her wedge heels. They were comfortable enough for a day at work, but when she'd gotten dressed this morning, she hadn't planned on traipsing around an amusement park.

That must have been why Mackenzie had tried to get her to change shoes. Next time, she'd follow the cues.

"What's the next clue? Also, this better be some prize if they expect us to pay for stuff along the way."

The disgruntled comment flew out of her mouth uncensored.

"They included these." RJ plucked three tickets from the bag and displayed them. "Why are you so surprised by today's activity?"

"It wasn't on my list."

It pained her to admit, but the puzzle had blindsided her.

"Interesting."

She longed for him to expound on his cryptic statement. But after the way she'd been tearing into him, she was afraid to ask.

"What else is in the bag?"

She grabbed it, emptying the contents into her lap—two gold tokens and a sheet containing the coordinates and clues.

She held up a token. "What are these for?"

RJ shrugged. "We'll find out."

A SUV blaring loud Christmas music pulled in beside them and Cynthia, Ella, and Earl piled out. She and RJ exchanged panicked glances.

"Read the next clue, QC. I'd hate for them to beat us."

"I sit above my peers as me and my little friends survey the world below." She frowned at the paper. "What does that mean?"

"I don't know."

She turned her glare on him. "They're your sisters."

"And we haven't lived in the same house for over a decade."

His terseness hinted at an underlying tension. Did that have anything to do with the animosity broiling between him and his father?

"I sit above my peers." RJ stroked his chin. "We're looking for something tall."

Vivian groaned. "It's an amusement park. Everything's tall."

"Then I suggest we get started. We have a lot of rides to check out."

The screams of patrons assaulted Vivian's ears as they entered the park, causing her stomach to clench with dread. Nausea rolled over her as memories flooded her mind.

She drew in a noisy breath and wrestled the images under control. This was not the time or place—she peeked at RJ—or the person with whom to lose control of herself. She could have her breakdown in the privacy of her room.

She just needed to distract herself. To forget that she was in an amusement park. She repeated the first part of the clue. I sit above my peers.

"There." She pointed to the Ferris wheel. "That's the tallest ride in the park."

Her finger only had the slightest tremor, which she hoped RJ would chalk up to a mild fear of heights.

"We don't have to go on the ride if you don't want to."

The compassion in his eyes gutted her.

"What about the proximity rule?"

She focused on the sound of children laughing and screaming on nearby rides, hoping their joy would temper her rising anxiety.

He lifted his shoulders. "It's a game. We can sit this out and get them on the next one."

"No." Her competitive nature rose to her defense. Vivian stomped toward the queue for the roller coaster.

"Vee—" RJ touched her arm, his fingers sending a shot of electricity through her.

She stepped away. "I'm fine. It's only a few minutes. I won't die."

Although at the rate her heart was beating, a heart attack might be imminent.

"Alright, if you're sure." His eyes remained glued to her face.

"I am." She distracted herself by going over the list of events for the wedding. It was probably invalid, as she wasn't sure what else the couples had changed, but it calmed her.

She vowed to memorize the agenda at her earliest convenience. She wouldn't be caught off-guard like this again.

The operator clamped her into the pod and she squeezed her eyes shut, hands gripping the bench.

As the ride lurched forward, her body felt weightless, as if she were floating, while her stomach stayed anchored on the ground. Bands wrapped around her chest, squeezing until it became hard to breathe.

She was going to die. She would die on this stupid ride because she was too stubborn to quit.

"Vivian. Vivian."

She didn't know how many times RJ called her before his voice penetrated the roar in her head.

"Breathe."

What a stupid piece of advice. Wasn't that what she was doing? Her head spun faster until she feared she'd pass out.

"Hey," RJ's arm came around her shoulder. "Look at me."

She opened one eye and peeked at him. Pearls of sweat popped up on her top lip.

"Inhale." He took a deep breath, encouraging her to do the same.

Her lungs filled with air, and her panic receded. Apparently, she *hadn't* been breathing.

He coached her through a few more deep breaths. "Talk to me. It'll help you to forget where we are."

She chuckled shakily. "I doubt it."

His lips curved into a half-smile. "It's worth a try."

"I hate these things."

"Why did you come on the ride if you felt that way?"

"It seemed like the right thing to do."

"How often does your impulsivity get you in trouble?"

"I'm not impulsive." Her rebuttal was automatic.

RJ arched a brow.

Except she was. She'd said something similar to him last night when he'd chastised her for faking a boyfriend.

"I'm not usually impulsive." She amended her statement. She thought she'd squashed that trait years ago and was not amused it had chosen this week to resurface.

"Are you afraid of heights?"

"No." She didn't get dizzy or become afraid at any other time except on a roller coaster. "My parents left me on the Ferris wheel once."

She'd wanted to visit the amusement park because her friends had gone at least once and told her how fun it was. She'd begged and cajoled, saving the money she earned from doing odd jobs for her neighbors to buy passes for herself and her parents.

"How long were you on the ride?"

She shrugged. "Hours." Bile filled her mouth at the memory. "I was fascinated by the view and didn't want to come off. They went on to other rides and left me."

It was fun at the beginning. "After five rides, it became

nauseating."

She'd stumbled off the ride, thinking her parents would be waiting for her. Though why she'd expected that when they'd proven to be fickle was anyone's guess.

"I bet they greeted you with a lecture."

"No." Her throat tightened at the memory. "They were gone."

"What do you mean gone?"

"They left me."

RJ's hand tensed on her shoulder. "How long were you there?"

"All night."

A muscle clenched in his jaw.

"It's alright. I hid in a ride when the park closed for the night."

She remembered being aware—even as a scared child—that attempting to find her way home alone after dark would have been dangerous.

"How old were you?"

"Maybe ten."

"Your parents deserve to be put in a barrel and rolled down a hill." He curled the hand resting on his lap into a fist.

She laughed. "They're not that bad."

Incredulity swept over his face. "You're joking? No child should be left overnight in an amusement park. You could have been kidnapped. Or killed."

"But I wasn't." She covered his fist with her hand. "Even then, God was looking after me."

She'd never considered it before, but her heavenly Father protected her when her earthly parents had failed. He'd provided when they hadn't.

And we know that all things work together for good to those who love God, to those who are the called according to His purpose.

"He's still looking out for me. Look." She gestured to the view behind him.

RJ stared at her.

"Seriously," she pushed at his shoulders, but she might have been pressing on a mountain for all her ability to move him. "Hurry, before the car moves."

He reluctantly pulled his gaze away and turned. "A tree house."

"And now the second part of the clue makes sense…as me and my little friends survey the world below…it's a reference to birds."

Thank You, Lord. Now they could collect the second piece and put this horror show behind them.

Seven

Chapter 7

RJ helped Vivian from the car, her revelations ricocheting through his mind. The idea of someone forgetting their children and leaving them in a park overnight was mind-boggling.

He had tons of questions but sensed Vivian's confession was out of the norm. He marveled at how well-adjusted she was after living with those people. He suspected that wasn't her only experience with parental neglect.

"The tree house is in that direction." She pivoted and would have marched off if he hadn't grabbed her arm.

"Let's take it slow. You look peaked."

She didn't, but she had to be queasy.

Her eyebrows shot up. "Why, Mr. Porter, it's a wonder some lovely woman hasn't snatched you up and brought you down the aisle. You know what to say to a woman."

His lips twitched. "I'm saving myself for someone special."

"I hope I meet this paragon who gets to spend the rest of her life with such a charmer."

Her sarcasm assured him she felt better, but he flagged down a vendor and bought water. He handed her a bottle.

"Drink."

"I'm not thirsty."

"We've been outdoors for a while. The last thing we want to do is get dehydrated."

She took the bottle and sipped. "You're used to being in charge aren't you?"

He grinned. "It's the privilege of being an older brother." He drank deeply from his bottle.

She narrowed her eyes at him. "You're not my brother."

"No, I am not." His eyes roamed over her figure, and he allowed a glimmer of his admiration to show.

The pulse at the base of her throat sped up and RJ took an involuntary step toward her. She sidestepped him.

"We should get going."

He nodded, swallowing hard. What was he doing? He wasn't in a position to pursue a relationship with this woman or anyone else.

He was on the verge of unemployment. Not to mention she worked for his sister's soon-to-be husband. He gulped down the rest of his water and wiped his mouth with the back of his hand.

"Yeah. Let's go." He tossed their bottles into a recycle bin, wishing his unexpected attraction to Vivian could be as easily discarded.

The tree house was massive, with a wide wooden staircase wrapping around its trunk.

He remained at her side as they ascended, glad he could stay close in case she needed help. At least, that's what he told himself.

Vivian ran her fingers along the smooth baluster. "It looks like it belongs in a fairy tale."

He agreed. Colorful blossoms curved along the stairwell adding a faint fragrance to the air. In the tree house, RJ and Vivian spun in a circle taking in the wooden chairs and tables. The faint scent of cedar drifted through the air, lending an earthy, timeless quality to the magic of the moment.

"It's a dining area."

He marveled at the ingenuity of transforming the tree house into a functional space.

"This is larger than my apartment."

"Mine too," he admitted. "Is it available for rent?"

Her lips curved as he'd hoped.

"I doubt we could afford the rent."

He chuckled. "You're probably right. Let's collect our puzzle piece and move on to the next spot."

"If we stay close, we should be able to split up to search the space." She was walking away before he could respond. She bent to search the underside of a table.

RJ turned away from the enchanting view, sticking to the outer perimeter while she checked the inner. As he passed by a window, a bird chirped.

Instinct had him sticking his head out the window. He spotted a bird's nest under the ewes. Beneath the nest, an envelope was taped to the wall. He leaned out and removed it, reclaiming another fourth of their photo.

"Got it."

"Let me see." Vivian hurried to his side, snatching the piece from him, a slow smile creeping over her face. "We're halfway there."

"Yes." He caught a curl that whipped free of her bun and tucked it behind her ear. The thick curl was as soft as he'd expected. "Why do you restrain your hair all the time?"

He'd known her less than a day but he was certain that was the case.

She caught the curl, tucking it into her bun. "It's less unruly that way."

Suddenly RJ felt an urge to tug her hair loose, to watch it spill around her face. He wanted to brush his fingers through the fragrant strands. He cleared his throat.

"This is a great photo op." He positioned them so their faces were close, the amusement park in the background. "Say cheese."

The faint scent of roses drifted around them. He'd never be able to see a rose again without thinking about her, which would become distracting after the weddings.

The convergence of his and Vivian's paths was temporary and he'd be wise to remember that, regardless of how much his heart responded to her.

At the same time, he never wanted this day to end, because when it did, they'd return to their earlier role—polite strangers forced together temporarily. He'd do well to stop forgetting that.

* * *

He opened the door of Sugar Bliss Pastries for Vivian. The scent of sugary dough and baked goods drifted toward them.

"Hmm. That smells delicious. Can we get lunch?"

He checked his watch. "I'm not sure."

He wanted to stretch his time with Vivian, but that was counter-productive. He needed to pull away from her, not find reasons to spend more time with her.

Too bad he rarely took the easy way out. "Why don't we finish the quest and go for lunch afterward?"

Not surprisingly, the line stretched almost to the door. Vivian joined the queue behind the last person and turned to him.

"Do you think your sisters chose places where we'd have to join long lines deliberately?"

"I'm more curious about when they found time to plan this activity and make arrangements with vendors."

"Why do you think we've only spotted one other group so far?"

"Either we're in the lead or each group has different coordinates."

She grimaced. "Or we're so far behind everyone, they've completed the challenge."

"Perish the thought." His competitive spirit couldn't bear the idea of another team winning.

"Hi," Vivian greeted the server. "We'd like an order of dukunnu."

The young woman's eyes widened. "We don't sell dukunnu, Miss."

"Are you sure?"

"Yes, ma'am." The woman bobbed her head.

Vivian drummed her fingers on the counter. "Why did they send us here if the bakery doesn't sell dukunnu?"

RJ leaned forward, resting his arms on the counter. "Is there someone else we can speak with?"

"M-my manager." The woman cast furtive glances behind

her. "Please," she lowered her voice to a whisper. "I just got this job and can't afford to get fired."

"Alright," he checked her name tag, "Sandy. We'll order pastries if you'll get the manager for us." RJ pulled out his wallet. "We'll take two gizzadas and a slice of potato pudding."

"Ooh," Vivian pointed to the mango cheesecake, eyes wide. "Can we get one of those as well?"

He added it to the order. "Does that help?"

Sandy nodded. "Thank you. I'll get the manager. One second."

A minute later she returned with a bald man in tow.

"Yes? Sandy says you ordered dukunnu?"

"We did." RJ met the man's gaze. "My sister sent us."

"You must be with the Washington group."

"We are."

Vivian beamed at the man who pushed out his chest at her attention.

"Where's my token?"

"Here you go." RJ slid the gold coin across the counter, collecting the laminated plastic. "Thank you."

He paid for their pastries and handed Vivian the cheesecake.

"I'm going to put on at least ten pounds before this week is through."

"Today's calories don't count. Not after we trekked all over Greenvale acquiring these pieces."

"Only one section left." Anticipation raced through him.

After this, he could have lunch with Vivian, and hopefully store enough memories so he wouldn't be lonely when they parted.

Eight

Chapter 8

She couldn't believe she'd told him about her parents. She never spoke about them because her stories normally horrified people, and with good reason. Archie and Sharon Ebanks had been abusive in their neglect.

She'd learned at an early age to depend on herself, as her parents were unreliable. Was that why she'd begun believing the lie she needed to do everything herself if it was to be done properly?

Surprisingly, she didn't have the urge to take over from RJ. The man had taken charge of their puzzle game and she was confident they'd win if it were up to him.

She was glad Jacqui hadn't come, so she had RJ's attention all to herself.

What was she thinking? She stuffed a forkful of cheesecake into her mouth and chomped on it.

The smooth cheesecake melted on her tongue, its rich

creaminess enhanced by the sweetness of the mango.

RJ stopped at a light and glanced at her. "Why are you the only one having fun?"

She rolled her eyes, but offered him a bite of cheesecake. He took it gingerly between his teeth, licking the frosting from his lips. Her eyes flickered to his mouth, lingering on his full lips.

"Vee—"

A long horn blast drowned out whatever he'd been about to say. Good thing too, because she was not looking for a temporary relationship. She and RJ could never be more since they lived in different cities.

Mackenzie and Cameron made it work.

She ignored her pesky inner voice and continued listing reasons she should keep her lips to herself.

RJ was her boss's brother-in-law. That would make being Cameron's assistant uncomfortable if things didn't work out.

And they couldn't. Six days wasn't nearly enough time to fall in love. Love? What was she thinking? Women like her didn't fall in love.

She flew from the car as soon as it stopped, needing a reprieve from her thoughts. When she returned to Portsville, she'd go on a date...even if it meant signing up on a dating site.

It was obvious she needed a refresher on why she was single. Or maybe she should dine at one of the restaurants on the property tonight. Surely there'd be someone she could talk to who wouldn't make her heart race a mile a minute.

"Don't you want to hear the next clue?"

She pulled up in front of the craft market entrance. "I'm waiting."

His eyes bore into hers as if he'd read her thoughts. But how could he? For a moment in the car, she'd wanted to kiss him.

If she had, would he have kissed her back?

"Vivian." He took a step toward her, eyes intent on hers.

No, this could not happen. She plucked the paper from him and angled her body away. This man was messing up her carefully laid plans.

"I make the girls pretty. They fashion me in many ways. But in this place, I'm one of a kind." She pursed her lips. "An article of clothing?"

She stalked toward the entrance and came to an abrupt halt as the colors merged into a kaleidoscope. Jewelry, dresses, shirts, and musical instruments clamored for attention. Voices rose in a melodic blend of lively exchanges and laughter.

RJ's hand settled on her arm, and the spicy scent of his cologne pulled her in, tempting her to move closer. She wanted to rest her head against his heart and feel his arms close protectively around her.

"Do you see anything that could be worn in different ways?" His deep voice drew her out of her trance.

"A t-shirt?"

"No, it couldn't be that. There are multiple vendors selling shirts. We're looking for an article of clothing that can be styled in various ways but sold by one person."

She sighed. Just when things were getting easier, it became more complicated. She wound her way between the stalls, RJ behind her.

"Are we going to discuss what happened?"

"I don't know what you mean." She feigned interest in a pair of coasters featuring alligators.

"Sure you do." He reached for her hand. "In the parking lot and the car."

"I didn't realize men enjoyed talking everything to death."

Trust her to be paired for the day with the one man who wasn't content to pretend feelings didn't exist.

He grinned. "Growing up in a household with three women will do that to you."

A pang of longing swept over her. In her family, she'd been the anomaly. The one who didn't fit in. Her parents were perfectly content with each other.

She swiveled her head, searching for the solution to the clue and to evade RJ's piercing stare.

Please, God, I don't want to have this conversation.

She didn't need him to tell her they were ill-suited. She already knew.

A swirl of color caught her attention. "I think I know what it is."

She hurried away from him, glad for an excuse to halt the conversation.

"Hello." She smiled at the dark-skinned, middle-aged woman manning the stall. "We're with the Washington party. Do you have something for us?"

"That depends." A brilliant smile lit up the woman's face. "Do you have a token for me?"

"Right." RJ dug the chip from his pocket and handed it to the vendor.

Vivian tuned out the rest of the conversation, transfixed by a teal scarf. She stroked the soft fabric.

"Do you like that?" The vendor came to stand beside her. "It would look beautiful against your skin." The woman draped the fabric over Vivian's arm.

"I didn't walk with enough money." She made a mental vow to return later to purchase the scarf. "Thanks for your help."

She nodded and hurried away.

She was halfway to the car before she realized RJ wasn't following her. She stopped, careful not to look at any of the stalls.

Their merchandise was too beautiful, and she didn't want to disappoint another vendor or herself when she couldn't make a purchase.

"Sorry about that." RJ caught up with her. "Let's go."

"What happened?"

"Nothing. We have all our puzzle pieces. Let's get back to the villa."

"Alright." Vivian buckled herself in.

She was the most contrary person. Despite all the reasons she'd convinced herself she and RJ were unsuitable for each other, Vivian was disappointed their day was ending.

Foolish woman. Holiday romances weren't sustainable in the real world. Things fell apart once the pressures of daily life reached the couple.

The couples getting married this week were an exception, not the norm, and there was no reason to expect the unexpected to happen two years in a row.

Nine

Chapter 9

Madison and Xavier were in the living room when he and Vivian returned to the villa. Emmy held out a hand and her fiance gave her a chocolate bar. "Thanks for not disappointing me, brother." His sister grinned at him. "I told Xavier you and Vivian would win, but he didn't believe me."

Xavier shook his head. "How was I to know he'd figure out the clues before everyone else, especially considering his team was short?"

RJ rolled his eyes, not surprised Emmy had placed a wager on him. "I didn't do it alone. Vivian was genius at deciphering your clues, which were horrible, by the way."

Emmy smirked. "If they were too easy, it wouldn't be fun."

"True." He handed her the completed photo and, when she was distracted, bit off a hank of her chocolate.

"Hey!" Emmy closed her hand over the bar, snatching it out

of reach.

"It's only fair since I was the reason you won it."

"I'm going to my room." Vivian edged toward the stairs.

He darted after her. "You can't. Remember? We must stay within ten feet of each other until the others return."

RJ silently thanked his sisters for the clause that would keep Vivian close awhile longer. "Besides, we're having lunch."

He gave the uneaten pastries to Xavier and Madison. "Consolation prize. We'll be back in a few."

He grabbed Vivian's hand, ignoring his sister's raised eyebrows, fully aware she was curious about them. She'd seek him out later and pepper him with questions. He wasn't looking forward to it, but he also had questions.

He pushed the thought aside. That was a problem for later. Right now, he wanted to spend as much time with Vivian before she found an excuse to dodge him.

"Where do you want to eat?"

"I'm not hungry."

"Please." He gave her an incredulous look. "All you've eaten today were two croissants and a sliver of cheesecake."

He guided her toward the dining area. Her palm fit into his as if the Creator had designed her for him.

They'd missed the lunch crowd, but RJ wanted to be alone with Vivian. It took him less than five minutes to convince a server to pack a picnic basket for them. The server even tucked a blanket in with the meal. RJ gave him a curious glance but asked no questions.

Outside the dining hall, he claimed her hand again. "I know a place."

He'd discovered the secluded beach the previous evening before hunger had forced him to search for food. It was at the end of the resort, away from all the amenities, which suited him.

"How did you find this place?"

"You're not the only one with secrets." He reluctantly released her hand to spread the blanket on the warm sand, setting the basket in the middle. "Can we talk about what happened now?"

She wrapped her arms around herself and averted her gaze. "I'd rather not."

He unwrapped her hands and pulled her to him. "You wanted to kiss me."

She snorted. "In your dreams."

"There too." He tipped her chin upward, waiting until her eyes met his. "I know what a woman looks like when she's attracted to me. But I'm curious, can you recognize the signs when a man is attracted to you?"

"I—" her tongue darted out to moisten her lips.

"Hmm. I didn't think so." He caressed the curve of her ear. "I imagine it looks like what you're seeing now."

Gentle waves lapped against the shore, their sound filling the silence between them.

"We can't."

"Why not?" He wouldn't allow her to push him away without understanding her reason.

"Cameron. Mackenzie…"

"Are getting married and much too preoccupied with each other to care about us."

"We live in different cities."

"It's not a marriage proposal, Vivian. It's an invitation from a single man to a single," he arched a brow, continuing when she nodded, "woman. Let's get to know each other this week, and if we agree there could be something between us, we'll figure it out."

He was doing an excellent job pushing all his problems away for his future self to deal with.

"Okay."

Her voice was so soft he needed to confirm.

"Okay?"

"Yes." She nodded.

"Great." He removed the hair tie from her curls. "I've been wanting to do that all day."

She smirked. "Did my hair tie offend you?"

"I was jealous." He buried his fingers in her hair. The curls were as soft and springy as he'd anticipated. "It got to touch these curls my fingers have been itching to."

She chuckled. "You're crazy, and now you've drawn me into your madness."

"Perhaps. But you should wear your hair loose once in a while." He pulled the scarf from inside his jacket. "Just as you should splurge on a beautiful item occasionally."

He draped it loosely around her shoulders.

"This is the reason you were slow to catch up to me." She fingered the vibrant scarf. "I'll repay you."

"Don't insult me, Vivian. It's a gift."

Hopefully, the first of many, as he sensed she hadn't received many gifts.

"It was my pleasure to get it for you. Shall we eat?" He gestured to the basket. "It'll give us an excuse to avoid the others later."

He'd have to speak with his father soon, but he'd rather do it when there wasn't an audience. Who was he kidding?

He'd prefer to sidestep that conversation for the rest of his life—a cowardly response for a man who'd spent his adulthood serving his country.

Maybe Vivian's suggestion for how he should approach his relationship with God could also apply to the one with his father.

He should run toward Robert Senior instead of away from him. Heaven help him, because confronting his father was scarier than going undercover without the proper backup.

But if he wanted peace in this life, and a shot at eternity, he must face his demons and vanquish them.

Ten

Chapter 10

Vivian stroked the soft fabric draped around her shoulders. She couldn't believe he'd bought it for her…or that she'd agreed to see if the undeniable chemistry between them could turn into something real. She must be losing her mind.

She studied RJ while he plated their meals on porcelain dishes.

The rich lived differently, that's for sure, because she would never have packed china for a picnic. But then, considering the rates they charged, they could afford to replace broken dishes.

"Why didn't you want to return to our villa last night?"

RJ flinched with his hand poised over the food. She held her breath, wondering if he'd deflect her question as usual.

He sighed, lowering the dish. "My father and I don't see things the same."

She waited, sensing there was more.

He scooped rice and peas, baked chicken, and sauteed vegetables onto a plate and gave it to her before serving himself. The delicious aroma teased her senses.

"My family owns and operates an antique restoration business in Cinnamon Hill."

She nodded.

"Since I was a boy, my father told me how eager he was to pass Forever Furnished to me. It didn't matter that I preferred playing sports or doing anything rather than learning the business."

He scrubbed a hand over his face. "That sounds ungrateful. I'm not trying to be. My great-grandfather Cecil founded the company because he loved history and restoring old furniture.

"No one was more surprised than Cecil Porter when people paid him to restore their old pieces.

"My dad loves taking what appears to be rubbish and breathing new life into it. He passed that gift on to Madison. What they can do is amazing. Even Mackenzie got some of that talent, though not quite the same way as Madison."

"How does Mackenzie fit in?"

"She loves the stories. She can tell you the history of every item we've acquired or sold. If the information isn't available, she spends hours researching after we buy it."

"She inherited your great-grandfather's love of history."

"Yes. She also has ideas for expanding and modernizing the business." He pressed his lips together. "My father's not a big fan of change."

Vivian set her plate down, her appetite dulled by the tightness in RJ's voice.

"How do you fit into the family business?"

"I don't." He gave a bitter laugh. "And not because Dad didn't try. He spent hours teaching me about different solutions and how to determine which one was right for each restoration.

"I endured the lessons because Dad tied it to my allowance, but left the business as soon as I was old enough."

"That's why you joined the army."

Her heart ached for him. It was difficult to bear the weight of someone's expectations when they didn't align with your dreams.

"Yes. I needed to figure out who I was. My father wanted to force me to become his clone. I didn't even get my own name."

"I don't know about that." She reached for his hand. "It seems to me as if you've taken Robert Junior and forged an identity.

"You're RJ Porter, the man who rescued a woman from an uncomfortable situation even when he thought she'd brought it on herself. He spent hours traipsing over town though he's in pain."

His eyebrows shot up. "How—?"

"We spent almost the entire day together, RJ. I've picked up on some things. Don't sell yourself short because you didn't become the person your father hoped you would."

"Maybe."

"I'm right and you know it. I'm certain your team would have more positive things to add to my observations."

A shadow flickered across his face when she mentioned his team. She was tempted to probe, but that was a question for another day.

"That's why I didn't want to return to the villa—to postpone Dad's lecture on building generational wealth. He claims that if children refuse to build on the legacy created by their parents, we'll soon have nothing left but new businesses.

"While I understand the need to pass things to the next

generation, I also believe that individuals should be given room to grow and use whatever gifts the Lord has given them."

"That's an uncomfortable position to be in."

"You're telling me." His lips flattened. "The disheartening thing about this debacle is that my sisters would love to inherit Forever Furnished and expand it.

"Dad is so focused on passing it on to me that he can't see how he's pushing Madison and Mackenzie away from the business they're passionate about."

"Parental expectations are a lot to deal with. But he needs to know how you feel."

"I know. What expectations did your family put on you?"

She huffed. "How much time do you have?"

"As much time as you need. I meant what I said." His grip tightened on hers. "I'm determined to spend time with you. I don't want whatever is developing between us to end here.

"I plan to coax you into giving us a chance, even if it means dating long distance."

She pulled back. "Aren't you moving too fast?"

"Vee, I'm a soldier. Life has taught me that sometimes you don't get to deliberate and make neat plans. You learn to trust your instincts, which sometimes means moving faster than the usual conventions. I'm sorry if I'm scaring you. I'll try to control myself."

"No."

No one had ever wanted her like that before. No one had ever pursued her with RJ's intensity. Her heart fluttered at the thought even as her head warned caution.

It would be interesting to see which organ won in the coming days. She suspected that when RJ made a decision, nothing stopped him from accomplishing his goal.

* * *

They returned to the Nutcracker to find pandemonium. The living room was full as members of their party gathered around the Christmas tree.

Vivian studied the controlled chaos. "What's going on?"

She raised her voice to be heard over the Christmas carols blasting from the television, but no one moved.

RJ muted the music, snagging everyone's attention. "What are you doing?"

Piles of ornaments and tinsels lined the floor.

"Oh," Mackenzie hopped up from where she knelt beside the gigantic pine. "It's time to decorate the Christmas tree."

She should have guessed there was a reason the giant pine was bare.

"The hotel provided decorations, but we figured we could make garlands from popcorn and cranberries."

RJ shook his head. "We don't have any stale popcorn."

"Did someone say popcorn?" Xavier entered the room carrying a large bag of popcorn. "We bought this in town yesterday."

"And this." Madison thrust a bag of fake cranberries at her brother. "Don't eat the cranberries, RJ."

"Ha-ha." RJ took the bag from his sister.

"Jacqui has needles and thread." Margaret waved toward a low table and couches at one end of the living room. "Why don't you two work with her to make the garlands?"

Vivian sat cross-legged on the floor. "What am I supposed to do?"

"You've never made popcorn garlands?" Jacqui asked with a soft smile.

The younger woman was pretty but seemed determined to blend into the background with her shapeless clothes and frizzy hair.

"Never," Vivian responded. The Porters and their friends were highlighting how lacking her childhood had been.

"It's easy. Here." Jacqui picked up a needle and showed Vivian how to push it through the popcorn. "The key is to aim for the center where it's more stable. The first time we did this as a family, we didn't know the popcorn had to be stale. Alicia and I ate so much of our supply we had to make more."

Alicia, Jacqui's older sister, had been Xavier's wife.

"I'm sorry for your loss."

Jacqui nodded, her eyes filling with tears. "Excuse me." She hurried out of the room.

Vivian watched her go, her heart twinging with sympathy for Jacqui.

"I'm never sure how to respond after someone has lost a loved one," she admitted.

"Me neither," RJ squeezed her shoulder, his warmth suffusing her.

The contact was brief, but his alluring scent lingered. She concentrated on stringing popcorn and cranberries.

"Why did Madison tell you not to eat the cranberries?"

"Because I almost did once." RJ chuckled. "The first year we used cranberry in our garlands, no one told me about the change. One of my sisters had put them in a bowl in the kitchen.

"I thought they were fruit. I grabbed a handful and popped them in my mouth before anyone could warn me."

"The red berries are lifelike. I can see why you believed they were."

He rolled his eyes. "The twins won't let me live that down."

She chuckled. "You love your family. I'm glad you have fond memories of them."

She suppressed her envy to enjoy the moment.

God puts us where we need to be, though we would rather be someplace else.

RJ's words from the previous night resonated. Being around these happy families hurt, but was preferable to her lonely apartment.

She closed her eyes and drew in a breath of chocolate-scented air. Her eyes flew open. "I smell cookies."

"We can't have a tree decorating session without Christmas cookies." Cynthia extended a platter with giant chocolate chip cookies to Vivian. "Want one?"

Vivian's mouth watered. "I shouldn't. We just ate."

"Live dangerously." RJ wagged his brows and grabbed a cookie, waving it under her nose.

The delectable scent of melted chocolate obliterated her defenses. She snatched an oversized cookie and bit into it. Vivian closed her eyes as the richness of the chocolate and sugar melted on her tongue.

"This is yummy," she spoke with her mouth full. "When did you find the time to bake?"

"We make time for what we love." Cynthia winked before hurrying into the other room.

RJ's eyes met hers and she couldn't tear her gaze away. He made time for her. Could she make time for him?

Chapter 11

The cookie was delicious, but RJ had more fun watching Vivian eat hers. Vivian's eyes fluttered closed as she bit into the cookie, her lips curving into a smile. Her appetite for life made him want to take her on daily adventures.

"You have a spot right there." RJ reached over and removed the smidgen of chocolate from the corner of her mouth. His pulse spiked as her lips parted at his touch.

He wanted to capture her lips with his. To have her long for him as she had the cookies.

"Are you guys almost done?"

He drew back at Mackenzie's voice.

"Not yet." He bit off a chunk of cookie, hoping to thwart any sly comments from his younger sister.

He should have known better.

"Concentrate on stringing popcorn instead of other things." Her eyes dipped to Vivian, a mischievous expression on her face.

RJ's face heated. "We're almost done."

"Oh-kay," Mackenzie said in a sing-song voice. "Cookies are tasty, but don't bite off more than you can swallow." She wagged her eyebrows before darting from the room.

"Let's hurry."

He stuffed the rest of the cookie into his mouth. Even the thought of his sisters or one of the others barging in on them wasn't enough to stop him from wanting to steal a kiss.

Heaven help him. The more time he spent with Vivian, the more he wanted to be with her.

* * *

The scent of pine hung in the air, the soft glow of the Christmas lights dancing off the glass ornaments. Their popcorn garlands added a touch of whimsy.

RJ stood on the opposite side of the tree from his father. He wasn't ready to take Vivian's advice yet, but time was running out. The storm brewing in his father's eyes warned him Robert Senior's patience was running thin.

Please, God, give me the right words to express to Dad how unsuited I am to carry on Forever Furnished after him. Help me do it without breaking his heart again.

Being a disappointment to one's parents was a heavy burden, one he'd lived with his entire life. But unless God softened his father's heart or gave RJ a passion for the business, it was a burden he'd have to bear for the rest of his life.

"This is beautiful." Vivian leaned closer, her flowery fragrance soothing his inner turmoil.

"There's only one thing left." RJ pointed to the pinnacle.

"Hanging the star."

"So," Cameron cleared his throat, "each family here has their own Christmas traditions. But we thought this year," he glanced at Mackenzie.

"We'd try something new." Kenzie slid an arm around his waist. "The youngest person gets to put the star on the tree."

Ella's eyes lit up in surprise. "That's you, Jadon." She stroked the two-year-old's head.

"Yay!" Jadon clapped. "I'm the baby."

Conner chuckled. "Thanks, guys. We were just getting him out of that stage." Conner brought his son to the tree. "Let's get this star up."

"We're not done." Madison flung up both hands. "The oldest person here needs to help him."

There was a whispered conference among the parents.

"That's me," Bob announced gruffly. "What do you say, Jadon?" He took the boy from Conner.

He'd forgotten that about his dad. Robert Senior may be a complete curmudgeon with adults, but he was a softie with children.

Bob gave Jadon his full attention. "Can we hang this star together?"

"I'm the star." Jadon clutched the star in his pudgy fist.

Vivian hid her smile behind RJ's shoulder. He placed his hand on her waist, where they fit perfectly.

"Sorry." Vivian jerked away from him, putting several inches between them.

"It's okay." He tried to focus on the drama over the star, but his mind kept drifting back to Vivian.

Ella and Conner offered the boy various items in exchange for the star, but the boy was adamant that he wouldn't release it.

"Mine." Jadon clamped his lips shut.

The toddler was the official ring bearer, but RJ hoped they didn't give him the rings. Neither of his sisters would appreciate it if the boy held up their ceremony.

He scanned the room, searching for something to distract Jadon. Finding nothing, he headed for the kitchen.

He spotted a sheet of cardboard and used a knife to carve a star.

"What are you doing?"

He showed her the half-finished star. "Check the cupboards for aluminum foil. I think I saw a package yesterday."

Vivian opened the cupboards, the wood clattering as she closed them.

"Here." She ripped off a piece of foil.

Working together, they wrapped the cardboard.

"Perfect." He grinned at her. "Now let's convince Jadon this is better than the one he has."

They hurried to the tree and RJ waved the star until it attracted the boy's attention. As he'd hoped, Jadon reached for it.

"Mine."

RJ jiggled the cardboard star. "Put that one on the tree and I'll give it to you."

Jadon reached for the tree. RJ helped his dad to guide the boy's hand.

Everyone applauded, prompting Jadon to do the same.

"Babies." Avery huffed. "They don't know what they're doing."

Twelve

Chapter 12

RJ's Bible reading plan took him to the book of Genesis. The story of Jacob and Esau always intrigued him. It seemed almost predestined for the twins to be at odds because of their stark differences.

Would they have been closer if their parents hadn't perpetuated the rift?

By choosing one child over the other, Rebekah and Isaac taught their children love was conditional and had to be earned.

This was how he'd felt growing up under the pressure of his father's expectations. As if he wasn't his father's son because he lacked a passion for antiques and restoration.

It was the complete opposite of Jesus' relationship with His Father. Before Jesus started His ministry, God claimed Christ as His Son, and He was pleased with Him.

You are My beloved son. Please Me.

Was it as simple as that?

Are you seeking the approval of man or God?

"You're right." RJ bowed his head. "Forgive me, Father. I want to please You and not man…including my earthly father. Give me the courage to stick by my convictions."

He wouldn't sign on for another term in the army, but his future wasn't in antiques. No matter what his father wanted. If only he could convince Robert Senior.

* * *

RJ limped into the main hall after his morning walk, hand pressed to his midsection. Each step sent a dull throb radiating down his leg, but the familiar ache reminded him he was healing.

"What's wrong with your stomach?"

"Dad." RJ dropped his hand and spun to face the accusatory voice. "I didn't see you."

He slipped the wood he collected on his walk into the pocket of his sweatpants. He planned to make a carving for Vivian.

"Hmph. Obviously, or you'd have gone the other way."

Guilt niggled at RJ. His father was right. If he'd had an inkling Robert was in the living room, he would have chosen another entrance or waited until his father left.

Parental expectations are a lot to deal with. But he needs to know how you feel.

"Can we talk?"

Robert arched a brow before nodding slowly. "I suppose you want to reject my gift again. My grandfather passed this business to my father, who passed it on to me.

"It is my right as a Porter to pass it to my son. To you." Robert bristled. "How dare you reject your inheritance?"

RJ rubbed the ache in his temples that was becoming a throb. "Dad. This is the reason I avoid you. I initiate the conversation and you accuse me of rejecting you. What about all the ways you rejected me?"

This wasn't where or how he had intended to have the conversation, but he had kept the words bottled up for too many years.

"Can you see me?" He tapped his chest.

"I'm looking at you, aren't I?"

RJ shook his head. "I don't think so. You look at me and see yourself. You see all the ways you failed and I'm an opportunity to make up for your mistakes.

"I'm not you, Dad. I'm my own person. I hate being cooped up inside, hunched over someone's dilapidated furniture. I don't care about a random family's heirloom.

"It could have been given to them by the Pharaoh of Egypt, I don't care. I don't want to spend hours sanding and buffing a piece of wood until it shines. I'd rather be outside in the fresh air doing anything else."

"It is the parent's job to create a legacy for their children."

"No." RJ's nostrils flared. "It is the parent's job to nurture his child and raise him to be the best version of who God created him to be. Children are not miniatures of their parents. Not unless that's their choice or what their Creator intended."

He took a deep breath, gentling his voice. "I don't care about antiques, but you know who does? Madison and Mackenzie. Emmy has your skill for restoring old items and Kenzie is passionate about the history and sharing it with others."

Robert Senior's anger smoldered in his eyes, but RJ was too far gone to stop.

"You have three children, Dad. Rather than forcing Forever Furnished on the one who doesn't want it and views it as a burden. Why not pass your legacy on to your daughters who love the business as much as you do?"

He walked away before he said anything more damaging.

Please, Lord, let Dad listen. My sisters would love to inherit the company. Let Dad see the truth.

Half an hour later, RJ took his usual position in the hall as his sisters and their fiances did the same.

"Morning, everyone." Emmy's voice was artificially bright. "Today's theme is family togetherness." Her eyes darted between RJ and Robert.

"There won't be any points awarded," announced Xavier. "It's about getting to know each other."

Great. He'd spend time with his future brothers-in-law to ensure the men were good enough for his sisters.

"We're leaving in fifteen minutes." Cameron picked up the narrative.

Jacqui raised her hand. RJ scanned her, surprised she was at the gathering. She'd missed most of them.

"Yes, Jacqui?" Xavier acknowledged her.

"Where are we going?"

"To the beach."

RJ groaned. He hoped there were miles of beach so he could escape his father's reproachful gaze.

By the time RJ made it outside, the rest of the party had left—except one. Vivian sat in a golf cart wearing a black and white kimono wrap and a floppy straw hat.

"Hello, Soldier Boy. Do you need a ride?"

The knot of anxiety in his chest eased. "You're the only person I'd accept a ride from."

She smirked. "Were you hoping we'd leave you behind?"

"Something like that." He sat beside her, tossing his towel over his shoulder.

"Shows how well you know your family. Your sisters asked me to wait for you." She frowned. "Though I'm not sure why."

"Aren't you?" He played with the curls falling loose at her neck, enjoying the way she shivered under his touch.

"They trust me to get you to the beach, especially since Jacqui jumped into the first cart available. I believe she'd have gone in the opposite direction if her father hadn't hopped in beside her."

"Hmm," he caressed the lobe of her ear, "my sisters are playing matchmaker."

She swerved and RJ clutched the side so he didn't fall out of the cart.

"No-o. They want to make sure you're okay."

He narrowed his eyes, his senses tingling with suspicion. "What do you mean?"

She parked in a lot crammed with golf carts and faced him. The salty ocean breeze drifted over his skin as he waited for her answer.

"You spoke to your father this morning."

He didn't ask how she knew, but she answered, anyway.

"We heard you."

He winced. It had not been his finest moment, and he'd have preferred Vivian not to overhear it.

She covered her hand with his. "What you said about your sisters was wonderful. I'm sure they appreciate it. I'm praying for Robert Senior to realize how he hurts his children by refusing to change his viewpoint about your family's business."

"Thank you. I appreciate your prayers." Perhaps he should

pray for his father as well.

"My sisters said there are no points today, but I'm sure they won't be able to resist a competition or two. Let's defend our title."

Thirteen

Chapter 13

Vivian strolled beside RJ, the salty air clinging to her skin, the warmth of the sand slipping between her toes. She replayed his argument with Robert Senior. He'd made several excellent points. A family's legacy was what they made it.

It was in the stories they passed on to their children. Their memories. By that definition, she didn't have a heritage.

Her childhood hadn't been nearly as idyllic as his. RJ's hadn't been perfect, but it was better than hers. Even with the strain between RJ and his dad, the Porters clearly loved each other.

How long had it been since she'd had a conversation with her parents? She'd gotten a job as soon as it was legal and moved out.

Thankfully, Cameron had been a generous employer, enabling her to survive without her parents' help.

RJ bumped her shoulder. "A token for your thoughts."

She half-smiled. "You don't want to pay for my thoughts."

"Come on," he tucked her arm through his. "You know all my secrets."

"I was thinking about family."

He pulled her to a large, white tent, a short distance from where their party had gathered.

"Is this about your parents?" He chafed her fingers between his.

"Yes, and no. I was pondering the idea of legacy, of what it means in different families." She laid a palm against his chest. "Your family loves you. This situation with your dad wouldn't exist otherwise.

"You have shared history and stories." A pang for what she'd never experienced caused her chest to tighten. "My family doesn't have that. The memories I have of my parents are the kind that make people want to call children's services or the police department."

A pulse clenched in his cheek, and she covered it with her hand. "Don't break any teeth on my account. I've made peace with my past. I'm only explaining so you can understand."

Her gaze drifted to the endless ocean, its vastness echoing her uncertainty. Gulls screeched overhead, their playful cries a jarring contrast to her distress.

Vivian gathered her thoughts. "If I ever have children, what stories will I pass on to them? What will they inherit from me?"

The thought was too depressing to contemplate further.

"Let's not dwell on it."

He grasped her shoulders, turning her until she faced the beach littered with his family and their guests.

"What did you say my sisters were trying to accomplish this

week?"

She frowned, struggling to remember. "They're blending their families."

"Exactly." He nodded in approval. "When you have children, you're blending two families into one. And maybe you don't want your parents anywhere near your children," he glanced at her. "I wouldn't. But family is what you make it."

"What if my child's father has a horrible family, too?"

He shrugged. "What if he doesn't? You can't live on suppositions."

She opened her mouth to object again, but he pressed a calloused finger to her lips.

"You get to create the family of your dreams."

Her eyes flashed to his, her heart speeding up. Was he proposing?

RJ smirked. "Now who's rushing things?"

He gestured to the people on the beach. Some lay on beach chairs, others had ventured into the ocean. The children ran shrieking on the sand.

"They may not share the same blood, but they're becoming a family. Vee, I don't know the full details of your childhood, though I believe it was more traumatic than you've shared. Even if we never become more than friends, I'd love to share my family with you."

Tears pricked her eyes, and she looked away, blinking at the sparkling water.

He didn't understand the gift that he'd given her. Women had fallen in love for less, and she was fighting to hold on to her heart.

* * *

Vivian knelt in the sand beside RJ, the sun pelting her back. As he'd said, his sisters were having an unofficial sandcastle-building competition.

Each of the Porter siblings claimed a portion of the beach and was busy crafting sand in their bid to make the perfect monument.

Vivian was glad to see Cameron kneeling beside his bride, sand clinging to his skin. The man had become almost unrecognizable—in a good way—since he'd been dating Mackenzie.

The twins had created impressive structures and were working on adding the details. Meanwhile, RJ was building blocks, similar to bricks, one on top of the other.

"You're doing it wrong." She checked the progress on all three castles. "Shouldn't you use a bucket to create the walls?"

She sank her fingers into the sun-baked sand, grains clinging to her palms, while the sea breeze carried the scent of salt and sunscreen.

"Woman," RJ mock-glared at her, "are you challenging the King of Sand Castles?"

"No, of course not." She lifted her hands in surrender. "I defer to your superior wisdom and excuse myself from this competition. I'll watch from over there."

She pointed to the beach chairs a few feet away. By the time Vivian repositioned the umbrella to shade her without obstructing her view of RJ, her position was taken.

Gracie and Avery knelt on either side, following RJ's instructions without complaints. She'd be sure to tease him about that later.

"He's wonderful with children, isn't he?"

Margaret Porter slid into the chair next to her.

"He is." Vivian clasped her hands, wondering why Margaret had sought her out.

"You're good for him."

"Excuse me?" Vivian stared at the older woman. "RJ and I aren't…"

Hmm. This was tricky. How would she explain their relationship? They weren't exactly dating, but hadn't they agreed to see where things went?

A mischievous smile teased Margaret's mouth. "I'm sure you young people have different ways of doing things, but I know when my son's interested in someone.

"You've had a positive impact on him. For over two decades, I've tried to convince RJ to tell his father how he feels about the business, to no avail. I've spoken to Bob about RJ's needs, but it never connected until this morning. The only new variable is you."

"I-I—" Vivian stuttered with the need to respond, but didn't have the right words. "I'm sorry."

"For what?" Margaret's eyebrows shot up. "For finally getting my two stubborn men to have an honest conversation about their feelings? No," she shook her head. "Please don't apologize."

Margaret reached for Vivian, her grip firm. "I came to thank you. If RJ continues to spend time with you, maybe my family will be together more often than at weddings and special events."

Margaret's sincerity touched her. How would having a mentor like this woman affect her? How would her children benefit?

Vivian pushed away the thought. This kind of thinking was dangerous. Because as much as RJ claimed he was interested in more than a holiday romance, she remained unconvinced.

It was easy to make promises in the heat of the moment. The real determinant was how a person behaved after they unpacked their bags and real life resumed.

Chapter 14

RJ surveyed his castle with pride. It stood six inches taller than his sisters' and was impressive.

"Excellent work, team." He high-fived Gracie and Avery. The girls had mixed sand and water at his instruction without complaint.

Sand clung to their skin, up to their forearms, but the radiant smiles on the girls' faces made it worth it.

"Come," he stood, holding out a hand for each girl. "Let's get you cleaned up."

RJ supervised as they splashed each other, giggling as they had a mini-battle. Their playfulness reminded him of his sisters and warmed his heart.

When they emerged from the water, they scampered away from him. He watched until they were safe with the Washingtons, then headed for his sisters.

"You made an admirable attempt. Sadly, you have failed to

beat the King of Castles."

"Oh, please." Madison rolled her eyes. "You cheated by putting your castle on a base."

He folded his arms and mock-glared at them. "Isn't that how I taught you to make castles?"

"Yeah, yeah." Mackenzie swatted at him. "Who has time to do that when they could craft a magnificent palace?" She gestured to hers and Cameron's with the flourish of a game show host.

RJ chuckled. "You guys are always too impatient to get started."

"Why are you wasting time with us?" A sly smile crept over Madison's face. "Go sit with Vivian."

His gaze shifted to her at the mention of her name. She and his mother were deep in conversation, their heads close together.

"I wonder what Mom's telling her about you?" Mackenzie mused.

Usually, his mother telling a potential girlfriend embarrassing childhood stories would stress him out. But he wanted to share every part of himself with Vivian. He wanted no secrets from her.

Except for the one where you're on the verge of unemployment?

His conscience niggled at him, and he brushed it away. Technically, he had a job. His leave ended on the second of January, so he didn't have to decide until then.

The thought of returning to duty plagued him with doubts.

According to the doctor who'd tended his wound, he could have died. He could have died and no one in his family would have known where he was.

Did he want to keep spending weeks, sometimes months,

away from his family unable to contact them?

The last time he'd missed his sisters falling in love and the discovery of his niece. What would he miss the next time he went on a mission?

He shook off the maudlin thoughts and forced a smile. This was neither the time nor the place for them.

"I'm going to rescue Vivian." RJ started for her, not taking his eyes off her.

"RJ, look out!"

He turned at Mackenzie's shout, but not fast enough. Someone barreled into him, a bony elbow hitting him in the gut.

The impact of the person's speed and weight sent him toppling backward. He twisted so that he took the brunt of the fall. The child was up in an instant, digging his elbow into RJ's stomach as he leveraged himself up.

RJ's stomach throbbed, the sharp sting of pain radiating through his muscles as he pressed his palm against the tender spot.

"Are you alright?"

"Who was that child?"

His family crowded around him, blocking out the sun. RJ threw an arm over his eyes, lacking the willpower or strength to force himself into a seated position.

"Stop crowding him. Let me pass." Vivian dropped to the sand beside him as his family made room for her. "Are you okay?" She pressed a cool hand to his forehead.

"I'm fine." His voice came out strangled. Admitting that he was in pain would lead to questions he couldn't answer.

Vivian stood. "Alright, people. There's nothing to see here. Give the man some room. He'll be fine."

The crowd parted with mumbles and RJ drew in a shallow

breath, grateful that she'd shifted the attention from him. His family kept watchful eyes on him, but at least they'd stepped back.

Vivian crouched next to him, covering the hand cradling his midsection.

"Does your stomach hurt? Were you wounded?"

RJ narrowed his eyes at her. "How did you know?"

"You grab your stomach after too much exertion. Have you told your parents?"

"No."

"Let me guess, it's a secret." Her lips flattened with displeasure, but she didn't wait for an answer.

"We'll do this in stages." She put an arm behind his head. "Try to sit."

It took two attempts with him gritting his teeth through it, but he managed it. With her help, he stumbled to his feet.

"Let's return to the villa."

"No." RJ gritted his teeth. "I'll sit on the beach for a bit."

She met his eyes. "It's not optional. If you expect us to be in a relationship, I have questions and you need to answer."

A combination of pleasure and dread filled him. He didn't want to talk about his past, but if he wanted Vivian to take him seriously, didn't he owe her a frank conversation?

* * *

RJ allowed Vivian to fuss over him, settling him on a couch and fluffing the pillows behind his head. He could get used to her hovering, the scent of sea and sand, with a hint of roses swirling around her.

"Do you need an ice pack?" She whipped up his shirt before

he could protest. She gasped. "That's a knife wound. A pretty serious one, from the looks of it."

RJ frowned. "How do you know?"

"I wanted to be a nurse and volunteered at the hospital for two years. How did you get stabbed, RJ?"

He winced. "I can't tell you."

She jerked back, tears filling her eyes.

"I understand."

"Vee," he grabbed her arm, preventing her from backing further away. "I got hurt in the line of duty. That's all I can tell you."

"Okay." She swallowed and tugged at her arm. "We'll be stuck here for a while, so I'll order lunch."

RJ panicked. She was saying the right things, but her frosty tone hinted at a death knell of their relationship.

"I was undercover. Things went south, and I got hurt. I was in the hospital for weeks. The doctors feared I wouldn't recover."

"Does your family know?"

"No. I can't tell them."

He'd always been vague about what his work entailed. They'd worry if they understood how dangerous his job was.

Vivian shook her head, disappointment on her face.

"What?"

"You keep too many secrets, RJ."

He was offended. "I can't share every detail of my life like some people. My job demands a level of privacy."

"Then maybe you should find another job."

It would have been kinder if she'd slapped him.

"What do you expect me to do? Work for my dad? Find a soul-sucking job I hate so I can have conversations about it?"

"No. Find a job you enjoy—work that fulfills you without ripping you apart. You claim your job keeps you from your family, sometimes for months."

She stood. "I suspect you stay away longer than necessary because you hate that there's a monumental piece of your life you can't share with them.

"Being a soldier is an important job. It's an excellent way to serve your country. But you need to decide if your job is worth sacrificing your family. And if you're content to keep lying to them."

Fifteen

Chapter 15

R J stared after Vivian's departing form as she stormed from the room. She didn't get it. He couldn't broadcast what he did for a living. He shouldn't have told her as much as he had.

Lord, please help Vivian realize she's wrong.

Is she?

The insistent voice of his conscience was unwelcome. RJ turned on the television to drown out his conscience and Vivian's words—to no avail. It was Christmas and all the movies centered on romance and family.

Every channel he switched to featured a couple falling in love or a family having fun together.

Had the resort conspired to have romance and Christmas-themed movies available on their streaming service, or was this a sign from God?

A bustle outside the villa gave him a second's warning before his family streamed into the room.

"There you are!" His mother's relieved voice caused a pang of affection.

"What are you guys doing back?"

RJ winced as he forced himself to sit up. He didn't want to show weakness in front of them. Not now.

"Did you think we'd be content to stay behind knowing you'd been hurt?" Mackenzie glared at him before plopping into an armchair.

"You don't have a good opinion of us, do you, son?" Bob skewered him with a piercing gaze.

"Of course I do, Dad."

Bob shook his head. "You said some things this morning that need to be addressed."

Emmy groaned and took a seat near her twin. "Is this the right time for this conversation, Dad?"

"When else are we going to have it?" Bob glared at his older daughter. "As soon as you and your sister get married, he'll disappear, and who knows how long it'll be before we see him again?"

RJ squirmed under the impact of his father's words. Perhaps Vivian was right. His secrets and absence were destroying his family.

Bob cleared his throat. "You were right."

"Excuse me?" RJ blinked at his father.

Bob's scowl deepened. "You heard me."

RJ glanced at his sisters. Their open-mouthed expressions convinced him he hadn't misheard. Robert Porter Senior was always right—even when he wasn't.

"What was I right about?"

"I have three children. I shouldn't have put the burden of

carrying on the family business on your shoulders alone." Bob pressed his lips together. "Though I suppose it's too late now with them, marrying men who live in other towns."

"Not necessarily." Madison crossed the room to lay a palm on Bob's arm. "Xavier and I discussed it. He can work from anywhere, but I have to be in Cinnamon Hill. After the wedding, we're buying a house there."

"Cameron and I will be close for a while, too. He's buying several properties in the area and it'll take a while to finalize the sales.

"We'll live in Ezra's house, and I'll work at Forever Furnished while we implement the changes…when I'm not traveling with Cameron."

RJ's chest tightened. His sisters were sacrificing their comfort to be near their parents.

What had he done for his family? He'd shirked his duties, only working in the antiques store to earn his allowance.

He'd joined the army as soon as possible to escape them and only spent time with them when it was unavoidable.

"That's wonderful!" Margaret clapped. "It'll be nice to have my girls nearby."

"I'm sorry." The apology tore from his throat.

"What are you apologizing for?" Puzzlement settled on Margaret's pretty features.

"I should come home more often."

"No one's accusing you of anything, dear boy." Margaret rested a cool hand on his cheek. "You're serving your country. The people of Saturn Island appreciate your service."

Tears pricked behind RJ's eyelids at the unwelcome commendation.

He could have done better. He'd often signed up for

additional missions near the holidays, so he had an excuse not to return home.

Work hadn't kept him from home, secrets had. He grew up on conversations at the dinner table of shared experiences working at the antique shop.

Later, when Mackenzie became an air hostess, she entertained them with stories about her clients. She couldn't disclose names because of confidentiality agreements, but still shared stories.

He'd stayed away from his family because he couldn't share his stories and being part of their gatherings became more painful every year.

"I'm leaving the army."

Their heads swiveled toward him at his blurted confession.

"What?"

"Why?"

"Can you do that?"

His mother and sisters spoke over each other.

"Give the boy a chance to answer." Bob's brusque comment quieted everyone.

But with their attention fixed on him, RJ didn't know where to start.

"I got hurt on my last mission," he began in a halting voice. "I was in the hospital for weeks. The doctors feared I wouldn't make it."

"RJ." Tears filled his mother's eyes.

Madison wrapped her arms around herself. "Why didn't you call us?"

"I couldn't. Then I'd have to explain how I got hurt."

Disapproval pinched the corners of Bob's mouth. "You could have died and none of us would have known."

RJ nodded, accepting the blow. "It made me consider whether I wanted to continue my military career."

"What about your contract?" Margaret's brow furrowed. "I've heard horror stories about soldiers who break it."

"It runs out in the first week of January."

His sisters' weddings had given him an excuse to take his leave in December, but the timing was perfect. If he quit, he wouldn't sign another contract.

"What would you do instead?" Mackenzie's gaze flickered between RJ and their dad.

The billion-dollar question.

"I don't know."

"I'm sure Cameron—"

"No." RJ interrupted her. He didn't want his in-laws to hire him out of pity.

What did he want?

Find a job you enjoy—work that fulfills you without ripping you apart.

"Don't worry about me. I'll figure it out."

He gave a self-deprecating laugh. At thirty-four years old, RJ didn't know what he wanted to be when he grew up.

"Sounds to me like you need to spend some time in prayer." Bob lay a hand on RJ's shoulder. "Let us pray with you, son, so you can find the answers you need."

For the second time that day, his family crowded around him. But this time, RJ didn't feel hedged in.

He'd shared one of his secrets and they hadn't rejected him. Instead, they stood with him to offer strength and encouragement.

His family linked hands, forming a circle around him. The warmth of his mother's hand and the slight tremble in his father's grip grounded him.

"Almighty God," Bob prayed, "I lift my son, RJ, before You. He's uncertain of his next step. He isn't sure if he should remain in the army.

"But You are not confused. You know the end from the beginning. You knew RJ would come to this moment long before he did."

His father's familiar scent of leather and linseed oil reminded RJ of happier times, calming his inner turmoil.

"Show him the right path. Reveal the next step and give him the courage to begin the journey. He's stubborn, like his old man, so make it crystal clear what he should do. Amen."

"Thank you." RJ's throat was raw with suppressed emotion. He'd neglected this connection with his family because he'd refused to have an honest conversation.

He'd blown any chance he had with Vivian because of his pigheadedness. The thought of losing her before they explored the feelings between them made him feel lousy.

Please, God, don't let it be too late.

Sixteen

Chapter 16

Vivian was avoiding him. He'd suspected it when she missed dinner, but after she skipped breakfast, he became certain.

He headed for the outdoor spaces, starting with the pool. He stepped outside and took a moment to admire the spectacular view. The sun warmed his skin, its heat tempered by the gentle ocean breeze that carried the salty tang of seawater.

His sisters had chosen a beautiful location, with its pristine white buildings and well-maintained spaces. The scent of hibiscus and roses mingled with chlorine from the nearby pool.

He veered toward the pool house where Robyn was working on last-minute details from the wedding. Vivian was on vacation, but like him, the woman was a workaholic.

He found her pacing in front of the pool house, her expression uncertain.

A grin tugged at his lips. "What are you doing?"

She whirled, guilt written on her face. "RJ, what are you doing here?"

"Are you sure that's the right question?" He cocked his head. "I'm not the one banned from working this week. Or the one micromanaging the wedding planner."

She huffed out a breath. "What else am I to do for an entire week?"

"You're almost halfway through. Only four days left."

A cold knot formed in his chest—his time with her was slipping away, and with it, his chance to show her what they could be.

Thank heavens for meddling sisters and future-in-laws.

"I have an assignment for you."

Distrust flickered in her eyes, her uncertainty hard to miss. "What?"

"The twins ordered me to plan a pool party for tomorrow evening, and you're helping me."

She pouted, drawing his attention to her full lips.

"Didn't you hear? I'm on vacation."

She said the last sentence with a sneer.

"This job is Mackenzie and Cameron-approved."

She perked up. "What's the theme?"

"We need a theme?"

"Of course."

"Give me a second. Let me ask." He whipped out his phone and texted his sister. The phone chimed almost immediately. "Christmas family traditions."

Vivian's scowl deepened. "Great, the one thing I have no experience with."

Empathy for her stirred in his heart. "That's where I come

in." He slung an arm around her shoulder. "We've already proven we make an excellent team."

"RJ." She turned to face him, bringing her mouth inches away from his. "I—" her tongue darted out to wet her lips.

He traced the lingering moisture with his thumb. Her lips were soft, making him wish he knew whether she'd welcome his kiss or slap him.

"You were right about my family. I spoke to them last night about my injury. I also told them I'm considering leaving the army."

Her eyes widened in surprise. "I never meant to suggest you should quit. Is that what you thought I was saying?"

"You didn't. It's something I've been thinking about for a while."

Even before his injury, if he were being honest.

"I miss my family. I don't want them worried about me all the time. Or for them to get the news that I died in the line of duty."

Death was inevitable for every man, regardless of their career. But he courted death more often than most. It was time he stopped.

"My contract runs out in the first week of January, but I'll still have to go through the debriefing process and some formalities before I'm officially done."

"Have you prayed about it?"

He half-smiled. "You'd fit in perfectly with the Porters. That was one of their first suggestions. Will you keep my decision in your prayers?"

"Yes."

"Good." He interlaced his fingers with hers. "How about I teach you everything I know about Christmas and you help me plan a fabulous party?"

"Fine."

RJ's shoulders relaxed at her acquiescence. All he needed was more time with Vivian to convince her they belonged together.

Seventeen

Chapter 17

Vivian cast a sideways glance at RJ as he spoke with their butler. The best thing about renting a luxury villa was that it came with staff. It made the setup and food preparation portion easy.

They'd informed the staff about the party, the number of guests expected, and their theme.

The butler suggested a menu, which they modified to suit their tastes.

"That's it," RJ announced.

"You didn't need my help, did you?"

He'd managed everything himself.

"Sure I did. This next part requires going into town for the items unavailable on the property."

"Like what?" She'd like to see what the villa's staff couldn't procure.

"When Emmy and Kenzie were younger, Mom created a

system for us to get gifts for each other." A fond smile crossed his face. "Her motto was if you didn't make it, you can't gift it. We pooled our allowances to buy material and made gifts for each other."

"Aww. Your mother's a smart woman. That tradition was thoughtful and sweet."

Christmas in her family had been completely different. If she wanted a gift, she had to earn the money and buy it herself.

That hadn't stopped her parents from purchasing elaborate presents for themselves. They often forgot they had a child, much less remember to buy a gift for one.

"What's the plan?"

"We're combining my family tradition with another familiar one." He wagged his eyebrows. "Secret Santa."

Should she tell him she'd never participated in those either? In school, the budget was usually beyond her. When she became an adult, she'd heard so many horror stories about the practice that she'd never participated.

Vivian kept her confessions to herself. RJ wasn't the only one with secrets.

* * *

She had to give him credit. When he made a decision, nothing deterred him.

They visited craft stores, purchasing glue, construction paper, and ribbons. They bought markers, colored pens, and crayons. And gallons of glitter.

RJ seemed to believe glitter was the glue that held homemade crafts together. The three children in their party would have tons of supplies to take home at the end of the week. Either that, or they'd make some teachers happy by donating the leftovers to a school.

"One last stop." RJ parked in front of a stationery.

"Haven't we bought every craft supply sold in this town?"

"Pretty much." He grinned. "Now we need wrapping paper."

"I'm not entering another store until you feed me."

Vivian folded her arms across her chest. She'd foolishly not eaten that morning because she hadn't wanted to bump into RJ.

She should have eaten breakfast at one of the restaurants. But the thought of encountering her over-zealous would-be suitor from the first night had kept her near the villa.

"Let's make a deal. We finish the shopping and I'll buy you lunch."

"Deal." Her hand shot out to shake his before she realized what a mistake that would be.

His calloused fingers swallowed hers, his touch spiking her heart rate.

"You'll have to talk to me, eventually."

Nope. She didn't have to do anything but survive the next four days. Then she could return to her boring apartment in Portsville and begin the next phase of her life as a lonely cat lady. The idea was depressing because she hated cats.

She snatched her fingers from his and bolted from the car, almost tumbling over her legs. Holding her head straight, she marched into the stationery, whispering pleas and prayers under her breath.

They were done in record time, and RJ loaded the paper into the trunk with the rest of the items.

"Time to eat." RJ reached for her arm, tucking it through his.

The rich, tangy aroma of tomato sauce mingled with the

creamy scent of melted cheese teased Vivian's empty stomach. Her stomach gurgled as her mouth watered.

They placed their order and sat at a table near the exit.

"What's your plan for the gift-making? For example, do you expect the girls to make crafts or will their parents have to do that?"

She was rambling, anything to distract him from the conversation he was determined to have.

"I haven't figured that out yet. Maybe divide the group into teams?"

"Families would work best."

"What about you, Lea, and Heather? It wouldn't be fair to the persons here without their families."

Lea and Heather were the maids of honor.

Her heart softened at his compassion. Why couldn't he have been one of those selfish guys? He'd be easier to resist.

"You could put us in a group together…a kind of makeshift family."

RJ scrutinized her for a long moment before shaking his head. "You're trying to get rid of me. Why?"

She blew out a breath. How could she explain that the more she thought about the two of them together, the less they made sense?

"Just say it."

She blinked at him. Had she spoken her thoughts aloud?

"Vee, it's obvious you're upset. Why don't you tell me what it is and we can deal with it?"

"What happens when you return to…" she hesitated. "I have no clue where you live."

"Cinnamon Hill. I don't spend much time there, so I built an apartment over my parents' garage where I stay when I'm in town."

She assimilated that information. "I don't get you. You love your family but avoid them. You don't understand how lucky you are."

"I understand, Vee. I've always known being a Porter was a blessing. It was the weight of expectations I couldn't handle.

"As for what happens when we leave, we already discussed that. We'll make it work."

She scoffed. "Will you move to Portsville to be with me?"

"If necessary."

"I don't believe you. No one has ever made that kind of sacrifice for me. Why should you?"

"You're sabotaging our relationship because you had terrible parents?"

Her mouth dropped open. "That's not what I said."

"Isn't it?" He raked a hand over his head. "I'm sorry your parents were neglectful and taught you that you weren't valuable or important. I'm sorry my childhood didn't suck as much as yours.

"I wish parents and caretakers didn't abuse or neglect children. That every child was nurtured the way God intended.

"But you're mistaken about no one making sacrifices for you. Isn't that what Christ did? That's the whole point of Christmas. As horrible as your life was, it should have been worse."

She recoiled at his blunt statement.

"You should be dead. The same as me and everyone else on this planet. But Christ made the ultimate sacrifice for us. He was treated like a criminal—whipped and spat on because He wanted to give us hope for a future.

"But you won't accept that bright, glowing future Christ pictured for you because you're busy living in the doom and gloom of your past."

She blinked at the stark image he painted. Was she negating Christ's sacrifice?

"Where are your parents? Do you think they're restricting their choices because of you? From what you've told me about them, I doubt it. I bet they're somewhere having fun, completely oblivious to their beautiful, accomplished daughter. The woman who has locked herself in a prison because of them."

He gripped the edge of the table. "The saddest part is that you have the keys to free yourself. All you have to do is use them."

RJ's chest rose and fell as if he'd run a marathon. Meanwhile, she felt as if someone had shaken her until her teeth rattled. Her head spun with the riot of emotions rushing through her. Rage, disbelief, grief. Despair. Anger.

"How dare you say those things to me? How dare you act as though you know me? You met me three days ago. What makes you such an expert on my life?"

"You're pretty easy to figure out, Vivian. You're a woman who has convinced herself she doesn't deserve anything good because she had a lousy childhood. It's a pity because there are so many things ahead of you if you'd pull your head out of the sand where you've buried it."

She gritted her teeth. Vivian was so mad she didn't have the words to articulate it.

His phone rang, breaking the tense silence that hung over the table.

"One minute." He raised a finger and dug his phone from his pocket. He frowned at the screen before answering. "Hello."

He listened for a moment, his eyes fixed on hers. His jaw

clenched, and he covered the phone. "I'm sorry. I have to take this."

Eighteen

Chapter 18

RJ stalked away from the table, phone pressed to his ear. The last thing he wanted to do was leave Vivian, who would wall herself deeper in her tower of denial. He wished he could make her parents see how their actions had hurt her. Although maybe it would be better if he didn't. People like that never appreciated their impact on others. If they did, they rarely cared.

He sat in the passenger seat of the SUV, needing a private space for the conversation. The leather seats were warm after only a few minutes in the noonday sun.

"This is Coupe."

He'd earned the code name after outrunning his entire squad during training.

"At ease, soldier," said the unfamiliar voice. "This is Cypher."

His shoulders relaxed as his tension eked away. "Coombs, how have you been?"

He and Elijah Coombs had trained in the same batch and became friends. Elijah had been discharged two years ago when his parents died, making him guardian of his siblings. He'd started Sentynel Security.

"Good. I hear you got seriously hurt on your last mission."

RJ didn't bother to ask how Elijah knew about his injury.

"Are you thinking of getting out?"

"Why?"

Elijah chuckled. "I have a proposition for you. Business has been great in the past year and I've expanded. There's room for one more person on my team. If you're interested, the position is yours."

Could this be the answer to his prayers and that of his parents? Security work was not as dangerous as being undercover. He would have the stability he craved while using the skills he'd gained in the army.

"Send me the details."

"Same email?"

"Yes. How long do I have to let you know my answer?"

"A week. Two weeks, tops. I have new jobs lined up for the new year and need to get someone on staff and trained quickly."

"Alright. I'll get back to you."

He'd read the information Elijah sent, discuss it with his family, and heavenly Father. There would be lots of praying in his future.

He laughed humorlessly. Sentynel was in Portsville. What were the odds of God providing the perfect opportunity for him to be near Vivian?

Would she give them a chance after he'd decimated her with his version of the truth?

Chapter 18

Please, God. I don't know what the future holds for me. But if I'm meant to be with Vivian, please open her heart to accept my apology.

He had groveling to do. He'd spoken the truth, but could have been kinder in his delivery. RJ ran a hand over his face as he headed for the pizzeria.

The warm, savory scent of baking pizza wafted through the door, but the tension in his chest didn't ease.

He'd felt less fear embarking on a mission than he did as he approached the woman he was falling for.

Nineteen

Chapter 19

Vivian remained frozen for several moments after RJ left. Was he right? Had she shut herself off from people?

She did a serious evaluation of her life. She had no friends, not even a pet. When she wasn't at work, she counted the hours until she returned.

She'd accused Cameron of not taking any time off. But wasn't she a bigger workaholic?

She took her vacations but didn't enjoy them. She had no hobbies that entertained her. Vivian had nothing she was passionate about, except her job as Cameron's assistant.

What kind of partner would she make when she was such a one-dimensional person?

"Vivian? Is that you?"

Shock rippled through her as she recognized the voice. "Mom? Dad?"

Her head swiveled between them. Sharon Ebanks wore cream slacks and a nut brown blouse. Her freshly styled hair fell in layers around her face.

Archie wore the same colors as his wife but in reverse. His hair was more gray than the last time she'd seen him, but he was as distinguished as ever.

Her parents were obsessed with matching or complementary colors—always in neutral shades.

She glanced down at her rose-pink blouse. Was that why she gravitated to vibrant colors?

"What are you guys doing here?"

She hadn't seen her parents in years. Why did she have to bump into them today, of all days?

Sharon wrinkled her nose. "No, dear. A better question would be why are you here?" Sharon surveyed the room, nose wrinkled in distaste. "A woman of your ample traits should not indulge in fast food."

Vivian ground her teeth. It was the same every time.

"You're eating pizza." She pointed to the box in her father's hand.

Sharon tittered. "It's different for me, dear. I'm already married." Sharon wriggled her fingers so the ostentatious ring set glimmered in the light streaming through the window. "Archie accepts that I have more meat on my bones than the average woman, and he likes it that way."

Sunlight glinted off Archie's glasses as he squeezed Sharon's waist affectionately. "Gives me more woman to love."

Sorrow swept through Vivian. Her parents' love for each other was so consuming that it left no room for anyone else—not even for her.

This was the type of relationship RJ wanted her to risk her

heart for?

Muted conversations swirled around them, heightening her agitation.

She may live with her head in the sand, as he claimed, but at least she was safe. She never had to worry about being neglected or fear that her children would relive her experiences.

What you're seeing isn't love.

Wasn't it? It was the only type of love she had ever experienced. The lie niggled at her conscience.

What about Cameron and Mackenzie? Or Madison and Xavier? Or any of the couples she'd spent time with this week? They'd made room for her in their family.

Love never fails.

What if RJ was right, and she had the keys to free herself from the unrealistic expectations of her painful childhood?

"Well," Sharon pursed her lips, "I suppose everyone deserves a treat. As long as you're doing it in moderation." She ran a hand over her ample hips. "We'll be walking an extra mile this evening to account for all these carbs."

Vivian suppressed her snort. Her mother's idea of exercise was to pull up a video and watch from the couch. The uncharitable thought niggled at her conscience.

She had no clue if that remained true. And if so, it wasn't her place to judge.

"I'm not eating an entire pizza by myself."

"That's nice, dear." Sharon glanced toward the door, her interest in Vivian waning.

The server delivered their order at that moment.

Sharon gasped. "Vivian! It's like you're determined to remain single." She wagged her finger. "What did I tell you? The chunky girl never gets the guy."

"I'm not eating this by myself," Vivian spoke through clenched teeth, aware that Sharon's outburst had attracted attention. "I'm having lunch with a…friend."

A low chuckle sounded behind her. RJ rested a hand on her shoulder, his intoxicating fragrance enveloping her.

"Come now, sweetheart. I thought we were more to each other than friends."

His fingers traced gentle circles on her neck, sending a comforting warmth down her spine.

"Aren't you going to introduce me?"

Vivian's heart sank. After his harsh statements, this introduction would confirm the death of their fledgling relationship. Perhaps it was best if he found out how horrible the Ebanks truly were.

"RJ, these are my parents, Sharon and Archie."

Twenty

Chapter 20

It took all RJ's self-control not to leap across the table and give Sharon Ebanks a firm shake. He recognized her type. She was a bully, and her husband was too afraid of her to do anything. Or maybe he was also a bully, the quiet kind.

He'd realized something was wrong the second he entered the restaurant because Vivian had curled in on herself, her shoulders hunched around her ears.

He plastered a smile on his face and extended a hand. "Robert Porter Junior. Archie, Sharon," he looked each of them in the eye, "I'm glad I got the chance to tell you what a wonderful woman your daughter is."

He gave Vivian an adoring look, brushing a comforting hand over her shoulder. "She's changed my life for the better, and I'm glad to have met her."

He refocused on them as they exchanged puzzled looks as if they couldn't understand what he was saying.

"Anyway," he drew Vivian to her feet, "we'd love to stay and catch up, but our friends are waiting."

He grabbed the pizza, grateful they'd asked the server to deliver it in the box. "Say goodbye, sweetheart."

He barely paused long enough for Vivian to waggle her fingers at the couple before escorting her outside.

He maintained a steady pace to the car, his concern for Vivian driving him. Her fingers were ice cold.

It was only a matter of time before she processed the encounter with her parents. He wanted her far away from the toxic pair in case she broke down.

They were at the villa before she spoke.

"I haven't seen them in eight years. I went home for Christmas and they stared at me as if I was a stranger. They had plans with friends and couldn't understand why I'd come."

She laughed, a watery sound that was almost a sob. "I spent two days alone in the house before I realized they didn't plan to return."

His heart hurt for the woman whose parents were so self-centered they couldn't see her.

"I always wonder what's wrong with me and why they didn't want me. I thought if I were perfect, they'd love me. I got perfect grades and joined clubs." Her face crumpled. "I received several awards, but I wasn't enough. I was never enough."

She turned tear-filled eyes to him. "How can you want someone whose parents think she's invisible?"

"Hey," RJ took her hands in his, chafing the icy fingers. "It's their loss."

She flinched.

"Yes," he hissed fiercely. "You survived despite them. You're ambitious, smart, and capable. I'm sorry about what I said earlier. I was out of line."

He hadn't fully understood the scope of her parents' neglect or the impact it had made on her.

"No, you were right. My parents built an imaginary cage, put me in it, and forgot about me. They were firm proponents of the belief that children should neither be seen nor heard."

"They're idiots." His comment startled a laugh from her.

"Perhaps." Her levity disappeared. "For years, I did their dirty work for them by staying in the box."

Her chin firmed with resolve. "No more. I'm busting out and won't let anyone trap me in a prison of their expectations."

"Good for you." He wanted to cheer or give her a standing ovation. He settled for beaming at her. "What's the first step?"

She blew out a tremulous breath. "Teach me about Christmas traditions."

* * *

RJ took Vivian's request to teach her about Christmas traditions to heart. Lucky for her, his family had many. It took mere minutes to convince them to indulge in some of the activities they'd have done at home.

Twenty minutes after accompanying Vivian to her room, he knocked on her door. She answered instantly, wearing a sleeveless mustard dress that flowed to her ankles. She'd left her hair free, allowing the curls to form around her face.

"Hi." His heartbeat sped up as if it had been hours since he'd seen her instead of minutes.

"Hi." Her gaze danced away from his in embarrassment.

"Vee—"

"RJ—"

They chuckled, and he gestured for her to speak.

"I'm sorry about earlier." Her hands flew up to communicate her agitation. "Seeing my parents was so unexpected, I didn't respond well. I didn't mean to dump on you."

He clasped the hand that fluttered between them.

"I want you to."

She cocked her head. "Want me to do what?"

"I want you to lean on me. I want to know what hurts or brings you joy. But more than anything, I want you to depend on me. Let me be the one you turn to when life gets hard."

He wanted that with all his heart.

She studied him. "You like challenges, don't you, Soldier Boy?"

"Sometimes." He skimmed a hand over her hair. "But being there for you won't be a challenge. It will be a pleasure."

A slow smile crept over her face, and RJ made a silent pledge to her.

He would be the man who built her up when the world tore her down. He'd remind her of how valuable she was when she couldn't see her worth.

Twenty-One

Chapter 21

"I have a favor to ask before we go downstairs."

She was still reeling from his bold declaration. "What?"

His eyes darkened. "Let me kiss you goodnight."

The passion in his eyes emboldened her enough to flirt.

"Why, Mr. Porter, what makes you think I kiss on the first date?"

"This isn't our first date, Vivian. We've been dating since the evening I rescued you from the buffoon at the bar."

She swallowed hard, remembering what they'd discussed, and the time spent together. He was right. They'd been in an intense, whirlwind relationship.

"May I?" His gaze dropped to her mouth, his eyes dark with passion.

Her lips parted in anticipation. "Yes."

RJ stepped closer until there wasn't an inch of space between them. He traced the contours of her face, his touch setting butterflies loose in her stomach. She shut her eyes, angling her face for his kiss.

His lips brushed hers in the lightest caress, but it was as if someone had turned the air-conditioning to its highest setting.

She slid her palms up his shoulders, appreciating the ripple of muscles beneath her fingers and the warmth of his chest against hers.

He changed the angle of his head, deepening the kiss, and her knees went weak. She gripped him for support.

This wasn't a simple kiss. It was an affirmation of her worth. An assurance that she was desirable. Treasured. Tears sprang to her eyes at the sweetness of it.

"Wow." RJ pulled back, chest heaving.

Wow, indeed. But she couldn't speak. The man had left her tongue-tied.

He ran a shaky hand over his head. "I thought I was being smart by kissing you so I wouldn't obsess about it all night. I was mistaken."

He took several steps away while she remained glued to the spot.

She almost regretted her request to learn more about Christmas traditions. She wanted to relive every moment of their kiss. Better yet, she wanted to recreate it many times.

"Come," he tugged on her hand. "Let's go downstairs." His gaze dipped to her mouth. "I'm fighting the urge to kiss you again."

Vivian allowed RJ to pull her into the living room, her lips tingling from his kiss. There had been an intensity in his gaze that she wished she understood. Perhaps later she'd find the courage to ask him.

The lingering haze left by RJ's kiss dissipated as she scanned the living room. The chatter from the Christmas movie mingled with the quiet laughter of RJ's sisters.

Margaret and Robert Senior sat cuddled on the loveseat, the older man looking more relaxed than Vivian had ever seen him. She stopped, leaning close to him to whisper.

"Are they supposed to be here?"

"Yes. I asked them to help us." He led her to a loveseat, pulling her down beside him.

She sat, shoulders stiff, shy in his family's presence, especially when she realized Gracie wasn't there and all the adults were couples.

"Relax." His warm breath tickled her ear.

"They'll assume we're together."

Hurt flashed over his face. "Aren't we?"

How was she to know? Her experience with relationships was limited.

"What I meant was," she gestured to Cameron, keeping her voice to a whisper. "My boss is here."

"Hmm," RJ stroked his chin. "I can see why that would be a problem. Hey, Cameron," he raised his voice. "Is it a problem that Vivian and I are dating?"

Her cheeks heated as everyone turned to study them.

Cameron smirked. "Nope. As long as you take care of her." He narrowed his eyes. "Vivian is important to me. I'd hate to get into a fight with my wife's brother."

Warmth started in her chest and radiated outward. Cameron would fight for her?

Maybe RJ was right. Family was what you made it and not limited to your blood relatives.

"See?" RJ slung an arm around her shoulders and drew her close to him. "Now you can relax and watch the movie."

She rested her head on his chest, enjoying the steady thump of his heartbeat beneath her ear and the warmth of his arm around her.

She could get used to this. "What are we watching?"

"It doesn't matter." Madison grinned at her. "It's Christmas—Hallmark movies are basically a genre. Pretty soon, all the movies run into each other."

Vivian frowned. "Then what's the point?"

RJ squeezed her. "It's the feeling. Nobody does Christmas like Hallmark. You'll see."

And she did. By the end of the movie, a grin had settled onto her face and her heart was a pile of goo.

Halfway through the second movie, the butler reeled in a trolley and the delectable scents of dinner became distracting.

Vivian ambled to the food station and filled a plate. She reclaimed her seat and bit into a chicken leg. Thyme and spices danced on her tongue, the flavors rich and vibrant after a long day without food.

She needed to take better care of herself. The on-screen heroine contemplated a permanent move to the countryside and Vivian groaned.

"Why is it always the women who end up moving?"

She'd watched less than two movies and become an expert.

"Exactly!" Margaret crowed. "My work here is done. Vivian, welcome to the family."

Vivian's eyes widened, choking on her last bite. She coughed, trying to dislodge it.

"Look what you did, Mom." RJ rubbed her back until she stopped hacking.

"What?" Margaret asked in a faux innocent voice. "Is it my fault you finally brought home a woman I approve of?"

Pleasure filled her even as her fear threatened to get the best of her.

"Drink." RJ handed her a bottle of water and she sipped.

"How many women have you brought home?"

RJ's expression became guarded. "Why do you ask?"

"Just curious." And jealous—extremely so.

"Ooh." Madison and Mackenzie exclaimed in unison. "We can tell you about them."

Vivian blinked as the two women's voices blended into one.

RJ glared at his sisters. "Remember your fiances are here and three can play this game."

Mackenzie angled her chin. "We're not afraid of you."

"Oh?" RJ leaned forward. "The summer we went camping when you were thirteen."

The twins gasped. "You wouldn't."

Vivian rubbed her temple as the women spoke in unison again. "Do they do that often?"

"Yes," RJ admitted.

"Sorry." Mackenzie smiled at her. "We forget how confusing it can be for people who aren't used to it."

"Let her get used to it." A teasing smile crept over Madison's face. "The way RJ has been staring at her, it's a matter of time before she officially becomes one of us."

Vivian slanted a glance at RJ, expecting him to be looking at his sister, but his eyes were on her.

"They're not wrong." RJ wagged his brows. "I have plans. Big ones."

Her breath caught in her throat. This man was on a quest to win her heart, and she was about to let him.

His family showed her that love didn't have to be exclusive. It could expand to welcome and make room for new people, the way the Porters and even Cameron and Xavier had included her in their circle.

Love is patient and kind; love does not envy or boast; it is not arrogant or rude.

The lesson finally clicked. Love was inclusive. It made room, expanding to draw everyone in, as the Porters had done for her.

Was she too much of her parents' daughter to change? Or could she learn to open her heart and allow love to transform her?

Twenty-Two

Chapter 22

Vivian awoke the next morning with the love verses running through her mind. She pulled up the Bible app on her phone and read 1 Corinthians 13.

"According to this, God, love is the most important thing." It made sense. God is love and His care for humanity reflected that.

She'd been a Christian for years. Ever since she'd watched a sermon online that said God was a good Father. Her desire for parental love had prompted her to pray the sinner's prayer.

She never missed her church's weekly service and sometimes attended one midweek. But maybe she didn't understand what love was.

If she had, would she have remained standoffish from the body of Christ?

"I keep expecting people to hurt me, Lord, because my parents did." She sighed. "How am I to become like You when

I fear I'm more like my parents?"

Vivian's actual fear wasn't that she was incapable of love, but that she'd become all-consumed with her partner. And wouldn't that be idolatry?

If she loved someone more than she loved God, didn't that make them an idol?

Fear can be an idol. You're so afraid of becoming like your parents that you undermine My power. You have put them—and your fears—in the place that belongs to Me.

Her mouth dropped open in horror as the truth of the revelation resonated deep in her soul.

"Forgive me, Father. I didn't mean to let my fear become bigger than You. Help me lay aside my fears and learn to love like You do."

Therefore, if anyone is in Christ, he is a new creation; old things have passed away; behold, all things have become new.

Tears dripped from her eyes as the words sunk in.

"I am a new creation." Her painful past didn't matter. Jesus had nailed it, along with her sins, to the cross.

All things have become new.

"Christ has made me new. Thank You, Jesus." She lifted her hands in praise.

The rap on her door startled her.

"Coming." She swiped at her cheeks as she hurried to the door. "Mackenzie?"

She frowned at the disheveled woman before her. "What's wrong?"

The pretty attendant's hair looked as though she'd raked her fingers through it several times and her blouse was buttoned incorrectly.

"Are you alright?"

She'd never seen Mackenzie this agitated.

"Yes. No." She ran her fingers through her hair. "Robyn's in the hospital."

Vivian gasped. "What happened?"

"Bee sting. She was allergic and didn't know. I'm on the way to the hospital."

"I'll come with you."

"No." Mackenzie waved a hand. "I hate to ask, but I need your help."

"Of course. Anything." Vivian wrapped her arms around her waist.

"Robyn won't be able to finalize the details of the wedding. I need you to take over. I know we promised this would be a vacation—"

"Mackenzie, I'm happy to help."

"Thanks." Mackenzie's shoulders relaxed. "RJ volunteered, but I'm worried he might miss a minor detail."

Vivian smiled. "Your brother's more resourceful than you give him credit for. Don't worry. I'm sure Robyn's taken care of most of it."

She reached out and unbuttoned the last three buttons of Mackenzie's blouse and refastened them.

"Get to the hospital and give Robyn my regards. RJ and I will take care of everything."

* * *

Robyn's detailed notes were easy to follow. The wedding was in two days and thanks to the planner's efficiency, most of the tasks were complete.

Vivian called the vendors to inform them to contact her

instead of Robyn if problems arose. The last thing Robyn needed was to worry about the wedding as she recovered from her ordeal.

Vivian was booking manicures and pedicures for the twins when the door opened. The savory aroma of garlic and fresh herbs hit her nose as RJ's broad frame filled the doorway. Her stomach rumbled in anticipation.

She gestured to a corner of the table where he set the tray and stood watching her while she wrapped up the call.

"How is she?"

"Alive." The relief on RJ's face was palpable, and she didn't take his comment lightly.

"Thank God."

RJ nodded. "He was looking out for Robyn today, that's for sure. Now that she's aware of her allergy, she'll keep Epinephrine on hand."

"Has she been stung before?"

Vivian found it strange that Robyn hadn't been aware of her allergy.

"That's the funny thing—she had. The doctor says allergies can develop later in life." His eyes met hers. "It's a reminder that we shouldn't take our lives for granted because something as tiny as a bee can cut it short."

So teach us to number our days, that we may gain a heart of wisdom.

He was right. She'd spent decades trying not to recreate her parents' mistake, allowing life to drift by.

She gestured to the tray. "What's this?"

"Lunch." RJ removed the stainless steel dome with a flourish, revealing lasagna and garlic bread. "I thought we could have a working lunch." He grinned. "Or a lunch where we didn't work and just talked. Your choice."

"Why don't we have a non-working lunch?"

He sank into the chair across from her. "I thought you'd never ask." He blessed their meal and glided a plate to her. "I want to run an idea by you. A friend offered me a job."

"That's wonderful. Is it work you'd enjoy?"

He nodded. "It's a security firm. I'd get to use my training, but the work wouldn't be covert, so I won't have to keep so many secrets from the people I care about."

Her heart fluttered at the intensity of his gaze.

"When would you start?"

"January."

He kept his eyes on hers. "I wanted to run it by you before I give Elijah an answer."

"You're the one taking the job, RJ. How I feel about it doesn't matter." But it was sweet of him to consider her feelings.

"The job's in Portsville."

Her mouth parted in surprise.

"I know Portsville is larger than Cinnamon Hill, but I didn't want to move there without letting you know."

"Is there a particular reason you want to live in Portsville?" She took a swig of sorrel, as her mouth had gone dry.

"There's only one reason I'd move to Portsville. You."

Why is it always the women who end up moving?

Her words from the previous evening replayed in her mind. "You'd move for me?"

"I'd do many things for you, Vivian. All you have to do is ask."

Twenty-Three

Chapter 23

Vivian had been quiet since he'd told her about Elijah's job offer and RJ didn't know what to make of it.

Would she be happy if he moved to Portsville? Was she hoping never to see him again after this week? He didn't know. He probed, but she'd clammed up tighter than an unopened pistachio.

Lord, I thought exploring my attraction to Vivian was the right thing to do. Did I misunderstand You?

Or maybe it was the job that was wrong. The uncertainty of his future unsettled him. The army was supposed to save him from his father's constant badgering about Forever Furnished.

In retrospect, running from his legacy was the wrong reason to commit to a lifetime of service. But what was he to do if he diverted from his career in the military and security was not his future?

Perhaps Vivian had the correct idea, and RJ should not be in a relationship until he figured out how to provide for a family.

Vivian cleared her throat. "These are the things I want you to finalize for the wedding." She handed him a sheet of paper.

RJ scanned the list.

Oversee the last suit fitting for the grooms, groomsmen, and best men. Collect money for vendors. Check with the father of the bride and best men about their speeches. Call the officiant to confirm selected readings.

"What will you do in the interim?"

She refused to meet his gaze. "Similar things, but with Mackenzie, Madison, and your mom."

"Ah. His and hers lists." If he'd wanted confirmation of her feelings, this was it. They had two days left at the villa and she planned to spend most of them away from him. "Got it."

He stalked toward the exit.

"RJ."

He stopped as if she'd given him a command.

"I don't know how to be the woman you want."

He rested a palm on the doorjamb. "That's the thing, QC. You're already the woman I want. The only person left to realize it is you."

* * *

RJ could follow orders. He checked off each item on Vivian's list while arguing in his head with the woman.

Why wouldn't she give them a chance? His temples throbbed as frustration built inside him.

They'd known each other for a short time, but it had been quality time. Their forced proximity made the four days more like weeks.

He clenched his fists. She already annoyed him as if they'd been married for years.

He shrugged into his suit, the crisp fabric cool against his skin, and ran a hand over his short hair, giving the olive and cream dressing room a cursory glance.

The sooner he finished this task, the sooner he could move on to the next.

"You're tense." Cameron glanced at him.

"I'm fine." RJ studied himself in the full-length mirror. The gray suit he was wearing for his sisters' weddings fit and that was all he cared about.

"Hmm." Xavier grinned at Cameron. "I remember those days. The right woman is worth fighting for."

"I know that." The words exploded from his mouth. "I'm trying to convince the woman to let me fight for her."

"Rejection hurts." Cameron lay a hand on RJ's shoulder, sympathy emanating from him. "But sometimes, when people have a difficult past, they don't mean to push you away."

RJ shot Cameron a look. "Do you know what she went through?"

He assumed he'd been the first man Vivian had told about her turbulent past. His shoulders slumped. Guess he wasn't as special as he thought.

"Yes, and no. I thought she was too young when she applied for the job." Cameron half-smiled. "Ironic, since we were the same age. I had her investigated. The reports were…"

Cameron's nostrils flared. "Let's just say it took a lot of restraint not to see those people punished for their treatment of her."

RJ understood.

"It's disturbing that no one called the authorities on her

parents."

"Yeah." RJ clenched his teeth. "Sadly, people don't realize neglect is as destructive as physical abuse."

"What I'm saying is," Cameron exhaled. "Vivian won't hand her heart to you. You must prove yourself worthy of her love. Then she'll open up. Once she does, take extra-special care of her heart."

"How do I convince her to trust me?" To love him.

"Break down her defenses," Xavier suggested, with a gleam in his eyes. "But do it with care. You don't want to create more damage."

Prove himself worthy. Break down her defenses. Don't hurt her.

The advice repeated on a loop but didn't help. He needed a coherent plan of action as time was running out.

In two days, his sisters were marrying their princes. If he didn't act fast, his princess would disappear forever.

"Thanks for your advice, guys."

Cameron must have picked up on his sarcasm because he smirked. "Alright, soldier. I'll give you some practical help."

Cameron pulled out his cell phone, fingers flying over the keypad. "Usually, I'd ask Vivian to do this, but considering the circumstances, I'll do it myself."

RJ's phone chimed with an incoming message.

"Don't be late for your appointment."

Twenty-Four

Chapter 24

Vivian accompanied the twins to the spa. "I don't know why you couldn't have come by yourselves."

She had booked mani-pedis for them.

Mackenzie arched her brow. "Robyn would have come with us. You're our temporary wedding planner, right?"

She didn't think that was how it worked, but Vivian buttoned her lips. In a matter of days, Mackenzie was marrying her boss.

She would keep her mouth shut until she figured out how that affected their dynamics.

Madison smiled at the receptionist, a young woman in the villa's cerulean blue uniform.

"Hello. The Porter party, here for our massage."

"Massage?" Vivian looked at the two women. "I thought you were having mani-pedis?"

"We called and rescheduled."

Twin expressions of mischief stared back at her.

"Of course," the receptionist smiled. "They're waiting for you in rooms 1, 2 and 3." The receptionist handed a paper to Madison and gave her directions.

"That's my cue to leave." Vivian pivoted.

"Oh, no."

Mackenzie and Madison each grabbed an arm. "You're coming with us."

"Isn't this your couple's massage?" According to Robyn's notes, it should be.

"They offer individual massages too." Madison knocked on the door of the first room they came to. A middle-aged woman in blue opened the door.

"Yes?" The masseuse arched her brow.

"Vivian Ebanks is here for her massage," Mackenzie whispered.

"Of course." The masseuse opened the door wider. "We were expecting you."

Vivian's eyebrows shot up. "We?"

The twins pushed her inside.

"I'm afraid there's been some mistake." She grabbed the door handle and twisted it, but it didn't budge. "This isn't funny, ladies."

Mackenzie or Madison chuckled.

"It's for your own good. We've paid for the massage, Vivian. Now, please, do yourself a favor and enjoy it."

"Wouldn't you like someone to knead away the stiffness in your shoulders?" Madison cajoled.

She had been tense since the conversation with RJ. A massage would give her time to think while she decided how to respond.

Having someone move to a new town to be with you was entertaining in a movie. But in real life, it was not to be taken lightly.

What if RJ moved to Portsville and things didn't work out?

Vivian groaned. "Fine. I'll stay for the massage." It would be nice to be pampered for a change. Who knew when she'd get such an opportunity again?

Vivian glanced at the masseuse's name tag. "Thanks, Fern. I'm sorry I made such a big deal."

The masseuse beamed at her. "I'm glad you agreed to the massage, Miss Vivian." She pointed to a pale blue door. "Please remove your outer clothing in that room. You'll find a robe inside."

Vivian lay on the massage table face-first at the masseuse's request. Fern covered her with a sheet that settled on her cool skin.

"Relax," Fern coaxed in a soothing voice. "Is there anywhere you want me to focus on?"

"My shoulders."

The scent of lavender oil enveloped her, calming her anxious thoughts.

"Very well. We'll begin shortly."

Fern pressed a button, and the wall receded to reveal another massage table with a man under similar draping.

Vivian's heart raced, panic surging as she stared at the covered form. "What's going on? Who's that?"

"Vivian?" RJ's shocked eyes met hers.

She scowled at him. "Did you put your sisters up to this?"

"No. This was all Cameron." He scoffed. "I should have suspected your boss was up to something."

"Miss Vivian, Mr. Robert, you must remain calm."

"You don't understand." Vivian's arm shot from under the cover. "There's been a huge misunderstanding. This man and

I are not a couple."

"We aren't." RJ agreed. "Vivian is one of those rare creatures—she doesn't need anyone."

A chill crept over her as the bitterness and pain in his voice hit her like an icy wave. "What's that supposed to mean?"

"It doesn't matter." RJ turned to his masseuse. "Please close the partition so I can get dressed and leave."

"No. We're talking about this."

He rolled his eyes, his exasperation clear. "Now you want to talk? Not this morning when we had privacy? You want to discuss this in front of two strangers?"

She squirmed under his scathing glare but didn't back down. Her instincts told her if they didn't clear the air, things would never be the same.

"I couldn't discuss it this morning. I needed time to process."

"You could have told me that."

"I should have." She sighed. "Look, if you want to be with me, you'll need patience." She gave a self-deprecating laugh. "Lots of patience. I'll pull away when things get intense because I need to process stuff and don't always know how to express that. Can you be patient with me?"

"I'd do almost anything for you, Vivian," he responded in a soft voice. "All you have to do is ask."

"Okay." She reached for him. "Let's have a couple's massage, and then we'll talk."

RJ clasped her fingers and her pulse settled into a calmer rhythm.

She'd use the massage time to figure out how to convince this honorable man she wanted a shot at forever with him. Even though she had no clue what that looked like or how to achieve it.

* * *

"So," RJ entwined her fingers with his as they strolled toward the deserted beach she now considered their spot. "What did you want to tell me?"

"I like you, RJ." The words slipped out and Vivian blamed it on the massage. She was so loose and limber, her entire body felt like cooked noodles.

"I like you, too." RJ stroked her hand with his thumb, sending shivers through her body. "What are we planning to do about it?"

"I'm afraid you'll move to Portsville and realize it's a mistake. That I'm a mistake and our relationship won't work."

"Hey." RJ stopped and faced her. "That will never happen."

"How do you know?"

"I just do."

She rolled her eyes. "That's not a reason. People break up all the time."

"True." He cupped her face, his eyes blazing with intensity. "But we can't live fearful of an unpredictable outcome. People break up, but couples also fall in love forever.

"We can ignore our mutual attraction and wonder forever if we made the right choice. Or we can take a chance and follow the path to the end. Perhaps we'll have an adventure that lasts a lifetime."

"An adventure." She tipped her face toward his. "I like the sound of that."

"All you have to do is say yes."

The yearning in his eyes convinced her. Was RJ the man for her? She wasn't sure, but until him, she'd never contemplated marriage. She'd believed she was content to remain alone for the rest of her life.

Yet, here he was, intent on pursuing her as if she were a damsel in a fairy tale and he was her knight.

"Yes."

"Best thing I've heard all day."

He leaned in for a kiss, and Vivian clasped his forearms.

She was ready for the passion this time. For the heat that swept through her entire frame. But the adoration caught her by surprise.

The way RJ cradled her, his palms firm but gentle—a declaration that he would protect her. That she was safe with him.

She sighed, pressing closer, her heart racing with the hope this man would cherish her heart.

Chapter 25

RJ whistled as he dressed. They had a crammed day ahead of them, but he didn't mind. He and Vivian were finally in agreement, and nothing would sour his mood.

They'd spent hours together, alternating between finalizing last-minute tasks and discussing everything.

He and Vivian had a lot more in common than he'd guessed. They were both goal-oriented, driven, and cautious in financial investments. They had a similar sense of humor and a passion for food.

He winked at his reflection, satisfied with his appearance, before hurrying to meet Vivian. He knocked on her door, grinning when she answered instantly.

She wore a stylish red jumpsuit with wide-legged pants. The bold color was eye-catching, while the soft fabric accentuated her curves.

"Are you as glad to see me as I am to see you?" He wagged his eyebrows.

She snickered. "Do they teach you corny pickup lines as part of your training?"

"Of course not." He mock-scowled. "That's what the internet is for."

She chuckled. "Oh, you're a comedian."

"No," he shook his head, "just a man falling in lo—" He coughed to cover his near snafu.

If moving to Portsville set Vivian on the run, what would she do if he told her he was falling for her?

"A man falling in…" she prompted, eyebrows raised.

"A man falling in love with Christmas and weddings," he improvised.

"If you say so."

His heart fluttered at her skepticism.

"Hey," he brushed his fingers over one of her springy curls. "Are we okay?"

"I don't know," she said with a frown. "Are we?"

"Yes. Why wouldn't we be?"

Disapproval scored her features. "I thought we agreed to be honest with each other."

"We did." Trepidation set his heart to hammering.

"So why are you lying to me, RJ? Falling in love with Christmas and weddings?" She propped her hands on her hips. "This isn't a Hallmark movie and I'm not a gullible woman falling for the charms of the experienced man."

He groaned. "You're right. You deserve the truth. May I come in?"

No way was he spilling his guts in the corridor where his sisters or any of the other occupants of the villa could overhear.

She stepped back without a word. RJ entered the room, shutting the door.

"I'm not in love with Christmas or weddings."

Her brows arched. "You think?"

He half-grinned. "I'm falling in love with you."

Her eyes widened as she took a tiny step back. "Isn't it a bit soon to be talking about love?"

He shrugged. "I can't help the way I feel, Vivian."

He'd always believed he'd know when he met the woman he was meant to be with. His attraction to Vivian had been instant, which caused him to put his foot in his mouth more than once.

"You don't even know me."

"Don't I?" He ran his finger over the curve of her ear. "I love how you care for others, putting their needs before yours. You get ultra-focused on a task, often forgetting to eat or care for yourself.

"You believe being your parents' daughter means you're like them."

She swallowed. "I've never admitted that aloud."

"You're nothing like the people whose genes you share. They're selfish, entitled, and narrow-minded. You are giving and caring…always ready to put yourself in the other person's shoes.

"Your compassion and ability to anticipate the needs of others is what makes you an excellent personal assistant. Mackenzie could ask for your help when Robyn got hurt because of your integrity and dedication."

She chuckled, swiping the corners of her eyes. "You'd better stop talking, RJ, or I'll get a swelled head."

"Impossible." He gave in to his desire and caressed her cheek.

"Is it any wonder I'm falling in love with you? I'm just a man, and you're everything I've ever wanted in a wife."

He may as well put everything out there. "I can't resist you. I'm praying that someday you'll feel something for me, too."

"I already do."

His pulse quickened at her whispered comment.

"It's not quite love, but," she lifted her shoulders, and it was the most encouraging thing RJ had ever seen.

"I'll wait." He stroked her bottom lip with his thumb. "As long as I don't have to wait all night to taste your lips again."

Kissing Vivian was at the top of his list of things he enjoyed doing. He could easily spend the rest of his life kissing her and never tire of it.

She rolled her eyes. "Well, we wouldn't want the assistant wedding coordinator to be distracted when he was supposed to be working, can we?"

"I hope not." He snagged her around the waist and drew her to him.

"Hmm." She wound her arms around his neck, her gaze lingering on his lips. "We have two minutes before we need to be at the chapel. Let's make them count."

"Yes, ma'am."

* * *

By the end of the wedding rehearsal, RJ had a new appreciation for Vivian's organizational skills. The woman could be a general in the army.

Yes, Robyn had done most of the prep work, but Vivian had taken up the mantle, relieving the pressure from his sisters, who could focus on getting married.

His mother tucked her arm through his. "This one's a keeper."

"I know, Mom."

She gave him an assessing glance. "Did I ever tell you how your father and I got together?"

"Only a million times. Though I can't imagine why."

His mother's claim that she'd fallen in love with Robert Porter at first sight had been hard to believe until it happened to him.

On a good day, his father's prickly exterior was hard to take. But then, he'd wrestled with his father's expectations his entire life and found Bob Porter more temperamental than most.

She laughed. "Your father may be gruff with you, but it's because he loves you."

"Yeah." RJ's eyes drifted to where his father stood at the altar, talking to Xavier and Cameron.

Bob was no doubt lecturing his future sons-in-law about how his princesses should be cared for.

RJ tipped his chin toward the three men. "I think I'll join them."

Xavier and Cameron stared at him in relief when he approached.

"Please tell me you're here to save us from your dad's lecture." Xavier pleaded with RJ in a manner reminiscent of Gracie.

"Why would I save you?" RJ stood shoulder-to-shoulder with his father. "These are my sisters. If you hurt them, I will find you." He lowered his voice in an imitation of Liam Neeson. "I have a particular set of skills that will make you pay dearly."

Bob grinned and clapped RJ on the back. "He'll do it too. My son's a Lieutenant Colonel."

RJ gaped at his father.

"What?" Bob scowled at him. "You don't think I know my

son's rank?"

"Uncle RJ." Gracie tugged on his shirt. "Are you almost done? Daddy says we're having a party. Avery and I are tired of all this grown-up stuff."

"Yeah," Avery chimed in. "It's boring."

RJ chuckled. "Alright." He took one of each girl's hands. "Let's have a party."

Twenty-Six

Chapter 26

Vivian checked her watch. They were on schedule. She exhaled with relief. Planning a wedding was more strenuous than overseeing the wedding planner.

Thank heavens Robyn was an excellent wedding planner, otherwise this would be much harder.

The wedding rehearsal went off without a hitch, giving her plenty of chances to sneak glances at RJ, who filled in for the officiant.

The man could set her pulse racing without saying or doing a thing. Apparently, all she needed was for RJ to be in the room or her brain to conjure an image of him.

She needed to concentrate. This was not the time to get distracted by the man sneaking past her defenses and into her heart.

Against her will, her gaze drifted to where he stood, smiling at Avery and Gracie. He was a natural with them, while she had no clue how to respond to the children and tended to avoid them.

"He'll make an excellent father."

Vivian started at the voice.

"RJ," Diane Washington gestured to RJ. "He'll make an excellent father. He's the type of man you marry."

"Excuse me? I'm not—we're not," Vivian pressed her lips together, flustered.

Why did everyone assume she had designs on RJ?

Don't you?

Her conscience was relentless.

Diane laughed and patted Vivian's arm. "Keep telling yourself that, dear."

"How do you know when someone is being genuine?" The words flew out of her mouth. Her cheeks heated. "Never mind. Forget I said anything."

She glanced around, searching for an escape before she further embarrassed herself.

"It's time for the pool party, isn't it?" Diane asked.

"It is." Vivian latched onto the excuse. "I need to ensure everything's ready." She backed away.

Diane grasped her fingers, arresting her movement.

"Let's go together." She tucked Vivian's arm through hers. "I hope you don't mind if we go at a slower pace?"

Vivian swallowed. How could she refuse the woman's request? Especially since the staff had set everything up before the rehearsal.

"No, of course not."

"Thank you, dear." Diane smiled. "Let's sit there until the crowd disperses."

Vivian arched a brow. She wouldn't exactly call their group

of less than thirty people a crowd, but she sensed the older woman had something to say. Better to let her say without an audience.

Vivian followed Diane to the seats before the altar and reluctantly sat beside her.

"Now," Diane turned her attention to Vivian. "You asked how to determine when someone is being genuine."

Vivian nodded.

"In what way?"

"If a man says he wants to be with you, how do you know…?" she trailed off, hands fluttering near her chest.

"Ah." Diane nodded sagely. "You consider the man's character. Does he keep his word? Does he have genuine friends? How does he treat women, including his mother?"

Diane touched Vivian's hand. "How does he treat you? You evaluate all those factors and then make a decision of the heart.

"How does he make you feel in here?" Diane pressed a hand to her chest. "But also in here," she tapped her temple, "and here." She touched her stomach.

"I don't understand." Vivian frowned at the older woman. "I should consider whether he gives me butterflies?"

Diane laughed—a delightful trill that made Vivian's lips quirk in response.

"Oh, dear. I can see I wasn't clear enough. Yes, butterflies are important. However, physical attraction is not the most important element of a long-term marriage. I meant trust your instincts.

"Sometimes, our gut tells us a person is not right for us and we ignore it. Then our hearts get broken and we wonder why."

It was sound advice. What would her mother have said in response to her question? Vivian brushed away the regret. As

RJ had said, her parents weren't worrying about her. It was time for her to stop obsessing about them.

"The man God created for you will value every aspect of who you are. He'll appreciate your mind and opinions. He'll safeguard your identity in Christ and help you live in ways that honor the Creator."

Diane leaned forward, a mischievous expression on her face. "If you're fortunate, he'll be an excellent kisser."

Vivian's face burned until she lowered her eyes, eliciting another burst of laughter from Diane.

"I can tell you've already discovered that for yourself." Diane stood. "Come, dear, let's not keep you and your young man apart any longer."

* * *

"There they are!" Avery and Gracie pounced on Vivian and Diane as they approached the Nutcracker.

The staff had arranged chairs around the pool, the faint smell of chlorine mingling with the cool evening air. Outdoor twinkle lights flickered on the walls, casting a warm, festive glow.

"Now, we can start." Avery smiled shyly at Vivian.

"What are we doing?" Diane asked.

Vivian shrugged. She'd left the games to RJ since he insisted it had to be extra Christmassy for her.

"Tell Robyn something nobody knows about you." Avery pointed across the pool.

"She'll read it aloud and we guess who it is." Gracie danced from one foot to the other in her excitement.

"Robyn's here?" Vivian searched for the wedding planner,

spotting her in the lounge chair near the villa. "Excuse me." She left Diane with the girls, making a beeline for Robyn.

"Hey," Vivian dropped into the lounge beside the wedding planner. "It's good to see you. How do you feel?"

Robyn made a self-deprecating face. "As if I almost died."

"I'm glad you didn't." Vivian reached out to clasp the woman's fingers.

Surprise swept across Robyn's face at the contact before she half-smiled. "Thanks. I hear you've been overseeing things in my absence?"

"Yes." Vivian chuckled. "I'm ready to hand things over to you."

"Oh?" Robyn arched a brow. "I thought you wanted to plan this wedding."

Distress flashed across Robyn's face. Uh-oh. She'd hurt the woman's feelings by micro-managing her.

"No. Robyn, you're an excellent wedding planner. It was easy for me to pick up where you left off because of how organized and detailed your notes were. I'm sorry if I made you feel I was trying to take over from you." She made a rueful face. "I don't want your job."

Robyn nodded. "Okay."

Vivian studied the woman. They were in the same age group. Could they have been friends if they lived in the same community?

A man who has friends must himself be friendly.

She pondered the proverb. Was friendship like love? Did people make room for each other, not based on geographical location, but because of a personal connection?

"I'm here to tell you a piece of trivia about myself." Vivian searched for an interesting tidbit to share.

"Yes?" Robyn prompted, fingers poised above her tablet.

"I'm an extremely boring person."

The children's muffled laughter punctuated her statement.

Robyn chortled. "That's your trivia?"

"No." Vivian rubbed her forehead. "I can't think of anything worth sharing."

Sympathy softened Robyn's expression. "Come on, I'm sure there's something."

"Nope." Vivian's shoulders slumped. How had she become this person?

"Can you sing? Dance? Juggle?"

"No."

"Are you a lefty?"

"Ambi."

Robyn gaped at her. "I hate to break it to you, Vivian, but the average person uses one hand or the other, not both."

"It doesn't seem remarkable."

She taught herself to use her right hand because her parents had been aghast when she used her left.

"I'm putting that down as your trivia." Robyn scribbled a note on her pad.

"What's your random fact?"

"Oh. I'm not playing." Robyn's eyes widened. "I'm the Trivia Master."

"Oh, come on," Vivian wheedled.

"Fine." Robyn rolled her eyes. "I can curl my tongue." She demonstrated. "My mom can do it too. It's supposedly genetic."

"Is it?" Vivian tried to recreate the action Robyn had done so easily, eliciting laughs from the other woman. "Okay, I give up."

"It always amazes me how much detail God put into creating

us. He pulls traits from our families, sometimes reaching generations in the past. Then He blends them into a beautiful tapestry. Take this family." Robyn gesticulated to the people around the pool.

"When they have children, some traits will be from people generations ago. They'll do some things simply because they observed it from one of their extended family members.

"They may never figure out where the trait originated, but each gets to use their gifts, their entire lives, to glorify God."

"I like that." She squeezed Robyn's hand before wandering to the group.

What if God would redeem the traits she worried about inheriting from her parents?

"There you are." RJ strode to her as she approached. "Is everything alright?"

RJ ran his hands up her arms, his touch sending a soft thrill through her.

"Yes, I was talking to Robyn."

"Is she well enough to take over?"

"Hmm." Vivian pulled away from him. "How interesting your first thought was that we were discussing the weddings."

Twenty-Seven

Chapter 27

RJ cocked his head, trying to identify the emotion he detected in her tone. "Weren't you?"

"Did you know I have no friends?"

Their words overlapped. RJ glanced around. His instincts told him she wouldn't want the others to hear what she said next.

"Let's get out of here." He lay a hand at the base of her spine, her warmth seeping into his palm as he guided her to the exit.

"Wait," she glanced behind her. "What about the pool party? Aren't we making Christmas gifts?"

"Later. We're working in teams. Candy Cane is crafting gifts for Reindeer. Nutcracker is creating presents for Candy Cane, and Reindeer is preparing gifts for Nutcracker. We've already decided on the ideas and gathered the supplies."

"I was gone a long time."

"Or," he winked, "we're efficient. The good news is that

there's someone in every team who knows about crafting. But that's not the point, anyway. We're not making perfect gifts."

"It's about the spirit of Christmas," she whispered.

"Exactly." He beamed at her.

"I was worried we'd crammed too many activities into this week. The wedding is tomorrow and we have gifts to make. We're having a party…"

She emphasized each sentence with animated gestures.

"We should have canceled the gift-making to ensure everyone gets enough rest tonight. As it is, they'll have to get up early for hair and makeup—"

"Hey," he caught her hands. "It'll be okay. Breathe. Tonight is about blending these multiple personalities into a family. We may have taken on more than we can manage, but so what?"

He shrugged. "If an activity or event doesn't get done, it doesn't get done. No one's putting us in the stockade for it." He shook her hands lightly. "It'll be fine."

"Alright. You may not know this about me but, I'm a perfectionist." She half-smiled. "I have a hard time when things don't work out how I planned."

"That works out well. I'm a soldier who loves a plan, but excels at improvising." He winked. "That's why God put us together. We balance each other out."

He swallowed the rest of what he wanted to say. Pursuing Vivian was the most intricate mission he'd ever attempted. If he pushed too hard, he risked scaring her.

But she wouldn't believe his sincerity if he didn't pursue her hard enough.

Lord, please help me convince this woman that we belong together.

The rightness of being with her had settled into his soul. She belonged with him and he wouldn't rest until he convinced her.

"Come with me." He extended a hand.

"Where are we going?"

"Can you trust me?"

She studied him, lips pressed together while RJ held his breath.

"Sure." She slid her hand in his, and RJ felt he'd won a medal.

He stopped to collect a basket he'd stashed by the Candy Cane pool before leading her away from the villas.

"You planned this."

She allowed him to lead her up the slope.

"Perhaps." He spread a blanket on the grass. The incline overlooked the property, giving them an overhead view of the resort.

He sat and drew her down beside him, draping a second blanket around their shoulders.

"How do you find these places?"

"The physical therapist suggested that walking would help my recovery. Initially, I walked to evade my father. Then, it grew on me."

She turned to him. "How are you guys?"

"We'll be okay." For the first time in over a decade, he could say that with confidence, and it was all because of Vivian.

"I've been spending time with my family. It's been great. I'm remembering why I like them."

She bumped into him playfully. "I'm glad. Family should be celebrated."

"There's always room for one more." He met her gaze, begging her to see what he was hesitant to say.

Her eyes darted away and RJ berated himself. Too soon.

"Why are we here?"

"Right." He pulled away, tucking the blanket around her shoulders against the chill night air. "I found out the resort's having a fireworks display.

"According to the brochure, if you look there," he pointed at the night sky.

Bursts of color exploded against the night sky as if he'd coordinated it. Vivian gasped.

"It's beautiful."

"Yes." He caressed her cheek. "There's a tradition about kissing at Christmas…"

She turned to him with a smirk. "Is there?"

"Hmm-mph."

"Pretty sure that involves a plant."

He produced a sprig of mistletoe and suspended it overhead.

"Why, Mr. Porter, you must have been a boy scout."

"Yes, ma'am. I believe in being prepared."

"Well," Vivian ran her fingers against his jaw, and her gentle touch sending his pulse into overdrive. "We wouldn't want your great planning skills to go to waste."

She leaned in to meet his lips, and fireworks exploded behind his eyes. He clasped her nape, fingers brushing against her soft curls. He would never get enough of kissing Vivian. Never.

Every second he spent with her made him crave more. More of her sweetness and warmth. More conversation and time. He wanted—no, needed—to spend the rest of his life with her.

"Vivian." He gave her one last kiss before pulling back. "I'm moving to Portsville. I need to be close to convince you to be mine."

"Good." She wound her arms around his neck, drawing him closer until his lips were a mere breath from hers. "I'm almost convinced that you're right."

* * *

Although his sisters were getting married the next day, RJ stayed up late. It was too soon to tell Vivian how he felt, but that didn't prevent him from showing her.

He'd show her through every touch, every glance, and with this perfect gift that she was the one.

The photo they'd taken at the tree house was his inspiration as he completed a carving of them.

As confessions of love went, it was pitiful, but until he was sure Vivian wouldn't bolt, he would keep his feelings close to the chest.

When he finally crawled into bed, it was past midnight, but the likeness of himself and Vivian was almost lifelike. He prayed that seeing the replica of them would open her eyes to how perfect they were together.

Please, God.

He didn't want to spend another moment away from his soulmate. And though she was in denial, he was certain she was the one for him.

Twenty-Eight

Chapter 28

Robyn approached Vivian after breakfast, her eyes filled with panic. "I need your help."

"Sure. What would you like me to do?"

"The florist's car broke down on the way here. Could you pick her up? I'd ask one of the staff members, but it's Christmas Eve and everyone's busy."

Robyn ran a hand through her hair. "I'd go myself, but I need to be on site to make sure everything runs smoothly."

"Robyn," Vivian interrupted. "I'm happy to help. Where did she break down?"

"Outside Silver Springs."

Vivian's brows shot up. "That's two hours away."

"I know. She called a tow service, but it's Christmas Eve." Robyn's shoulders drooped. "I don't know why I thought things would be easier with a destination wedding."

"It's okay." Vivian lay a tentative hand on the woman's

shoulder. "How will we get there?"

She assumed RJ would go with her.

Robyn gave Vivian her key. "You can use my car. Thank you." She threw her arms around Vivian and squeezed before dashing off. "Call me if you need anything."

"What was that about?" RJ came over after Robyn left.

"The florist is stranded in Silver Springs."

RJ whistled. "Don't tell the twins."

"Don't tell the twins what?" Madison and Mackenzie popped up on either side of RJ.

"That they're late for their hair appointments." Vivian improvised.

Mackenzie and Madison exchanged looks before darting away.

RJ leaned in after they left. "What's the plan?"

"Road trip?"

They updated Bob and Margaret before heading out.

"Alright." RJ turned to her when she buckled in. "This is the perfect opportunity to complete your Christmas Traditions education."

She rolled her eyes. But his commitment to sharing his family's traditions with her was touching.

"Your sisters are getting married in six hours and their flowers are four hours away. Christmas traditions are the least of our worries."

"This is important," RJ insisted, "and it won't take long. You'll be voting for the greatest Christmas album of all time."

She snickered. "That's the important thing?"

"Yes." He opened a music app. "We're starting with the great Boyz 2 Men."

The smooth, velvet tones of the singers wrapped around her

like a comforting blanket, making her feel at ease despite her usual disinterest in music.

Forty-five minutes later, RJ pulled into a gas station to fill the tank of Robyn's SUV.

"Well?"

"It was alright?"

"Alright?" He gaped at her. "It is the greatest Christmas album in at least fifty years."

She giggled. "If you say so."

He huffed. "I suppose you'll agree with my sisters' choice."

"The album's okay. Their voices were…mellow. Soothing." She laughed at his outraged expression. "I'm not a music lover."

"Everyone loves music."

She grimaced. "Not me."

"You haven't found the right music yet."

"Something tells me you're taking this as a challenge."

He flashed her a grin as he pulled onto the main road. "You're the one who threw your gauntlet at me."

She rolled her eyes. "Let's take a break before the next album."

"Fine. Why don't you like music?"

She shrugged. "My parents like music."

"So?"

Her response sounded petty…as if she automatically hated anything her parents loved. Vivian leaned against the headrest, searching for the words to express herself.

"Growing up, music was another thing my parents put ahead of me. They invited their friends over, listening to music until late into the night. It didn't matter what I had going on at school the next day.

"Their sole concern was their schedule. If they felt like having a late-night party, that's what they did."

"What do your parents do for a living?"

"They're computer programmers."

"Both of them?"

The incredulity in RJ's voice didn't offend her.

"That's how they met. They were partners on a project and realized they worked better together."

Her parents had a beautiful love story—until her birth ruined it.

"Their hours were flexible. As long as they completed their projects on time, their boss didn't care."

"I'm sorry." RJ reached for her hand across the console. "I wish your childhood had been different, but…"

"But?" she prompted.

"Would you have been as resilient if you had an easier childhood?"

"I've wondered the same."

"Count it all joy when you fall into various trials, knowing that the testing of your faith produces patience." RJ squeezed her hand.

They quoted the second half of the verse in unison.

"But let patience have its perfect work, that you may be perfect and complete, lacking nothing."

Count it all joy. She let the silence settle between them as she pondered the words of Jesus' brother.

If her home life had been loving, would she have left home at eighteen and gotten a job with Cameron?

Would she have spent the last eleven years of her life working in a position that fulfilled and challenged her?

If her childhood had been easier, would she have settled for mediocrity? Perhaps she wouldn't have pushed herself so hard in school. Or she would have dated and married a man who later broke her heart.

She studied RJ's profile. Would she have met this man who challenged her in the best ways? A man who appreciated her mind and encouraged her to be better. Diane's words drifted back to her.

The man God created for you will value every aspect of who you are.

"Do you think I'm pretty, RJ?"

She clapped her hand over her mouth as the words flew out without her consent.

He glanced at her with a smirk. "What do you think?"

She shrugged. "I don't know."

If she'd been confident, the question wouldn't have plagued her.

"Did you forget my nickname for you is Queen of Curves?" He half-smiled. "I considered calling you 'Beautiful' or 'Precious', but I didn't want to start a fight."

The way he said the words made her toes curl.

"You're gorgeous, Vee. I love—" His grip tightened on the wheel. "You're beautiful, inside and out. And if we weren't on a mission to save my sisters' weddings, I'd show you just how much I mean it."

Warmth spread from her heart until it suffused her entire body. No one had ever made her feel as if she was perfect as she was.

She wanted to change her past so she could give him a pure heart, one that hadn't become jaded because of her parents' neglect. But as they'd said, would she be the same woman?

Stop dwelling on your past. Release it into My hands and I can redeem it. I can redeem you.

The still, small voice whispered to her spirit and Vivian

realized she'd gone about everything wrong. She'd gone to God looking for a replacement for her earthly father, but taken her baggage along.

Though she believed burdens were lifted at Calvary, that Jesus had died for her sins…that she was a new creation in Him, she wasn't living victorious. She remained a prisoner.

RJ had seen it, but he'd only been partially right. She didn't have the keys to free herself. Christ did.

Vivian closed her eyes as she visualized Jesus unlocking the door to her cage. She imagined taking His hand, leaving her baggage behind. Hopefully, for the last time.

Warmth spread in her chest, slow at first, until it suffused her entire body. A weight lifted from her as Vivian realized she was finally free.

Twenty-Nine

Chapter 29

He couldn't keep his feelings hidden from Vivian much longer. He'd almost confessed his love, and then what would have happened?

She would have retreated so far behind her walls that he'd never reach her.

Lord, why'd You put Vivian in my life?

It wasn't a complaint. Being around Vivian had shown him how much he wanted a home and a life with her. He wanted to share his family's traditions and make new ones.

But could she let down her barriers enough to let him love her?

"Do you believe you're worthy of love?" He blurted the question, regretting it instantly.

This was not the way to ease his skittish sweetheart into seeing things his way.

"Funny you should ask me that."

"Forget I said anything. Let's listen to the second album."

He shouldn't have started this conversation while driving. He needed to see her face.

"RJ." She squeezed his knee. "I want to answer you."

"Okay."

"If you had asked me fifteen minutes ago, my answer would have been different."

"And now?"

"It's complicated."

He heard the smile in her voice.

"The message my parents taught was that I'm immaterial. Even at the pizzeria, they were completely absorbed with each other.

"My mother's major concern was not how I'd fared since the last time she saw me, but whether I planned to eat an entire pizza alone.

"You basically declared yourself as my boyfriend and they didn't have a single comment or question."

He'd noticed that. Had the situation been reversed, his parents would have had many questions for Vivian. They hadn't interrogated her because they had the chance to observe her and get to know her for themselves.

When he professed his intentions, Vivian would garner the unwavering attention of his parents and sisters. He suppressed a groan.

Please, Lord, let her be ready for the full brunt of my family before that happens.

"But the Holy Spirit reminded me of the reason I first attended a church. It was to find the type of love lacking in my family."

"Don't you have any other relatives?"

What were the odds of two orphans meeting and falling in love?

"No clue. If I do, I've never met them." She scoffed. "Given my luck, if they exist, they're just as self-absorbed as my parents."

He made a vow to find out. Vivian may not choose to admit it, but she belonged in a large family...

As much as he would love to make her a part of his family, she'd enjoy meeting relatives who weren't like her parents.

Please, God, let them exist.

"Anyway," she continued. "I realized that my two beliefs clashed. God created me in His image. Since God is love, I'm capable of the emotion and deserve to experience it."

He nodded his agreement, afraid to speak and derail her train of thought.

"My history and family say the opposite. They tell me I'm unworthy of love and should stop searching for it."

His heart ached for the woman who'd spent her life feeling unlovable.

She cleared her throat. "Since those ideas are opposites, one must be a lie. Since God is truth and cannot lie, my experiences have taught me a false belief."

He reached for her, needing to offer her a measure of support. She clutched his hand, her fingers trembling in his.

"You deserve to be loved."

"I know."

The two words reverberated in his mind. She believed she was worthy of love. Finally.

Tell her how you feel.

Beads of sweat popped on his forehead despite the vehicle's air conditioning. What if he confessed his feelings and she rejected him?

Tell her.

"Vivian, I—"

The chorus of Jingle Bells interrupted him. He glanced at her.

"One minute." She held up a finger, a huge grin on her face. "Hello. Yes. We're almost in Silver Springs. Where are you, exactly?"

* * *

RJ parked on the shoulder in front of a white florist van with the words The Fair Child blazoned across the back doors.

"This is it."

The need to confess his feelings pressed on him. "Vivian—"

"We'll listen to the album on our return trip. Promise." She opened the door. "Let's rescue your sisters' flowers."

"Right." He hopped out of the SUV and followed her. Today's mission was to save his sisters' weddings. He could secure his future with Vivian later.

Please, God, let there be a future for us.

"Sunshine?" Vivian waved to get the attention of the pretty woman slumped behind the steering wheel.

"Yes?" She cracked the window of the van.

"We're with the Porter wedding."

"Thank goodness!" Sunshine jumped onto the pavement, gravel crackling under her feet. "I was getting worried. I checked on the flowers five minutes ago and they're fine." She rolled her eyes. "Serves me right for buying a vehicle without having it checked by a mechanic."

Sunshine hurried toward the rear door. "Is the air-conditioning in your vehicle on?"

"Yes." Vivian trailed her. "How can we help?"

"Let's transfer the flowers to your car."

RJ opened the trunk before heading for the florist truck. A puff of cold air drifted around them as Sunshine removed the flowers.

"Here." Sunshine thrust a box with two bouquets sticking out of its center at him.

They transferred the flowers from the van to Robyn's SUV in three minutes.

RJ slammed the trunk and turned to Sunshine. "What should we do about your truck?"

"Someone called for a tow?" A tall, skinny man with a stringy gray beard squinted at them. A white name tag on his brown overalls announced his name as Rick.

"Sorry it took so long. You'd be surprised at the number of emergency calls we had today. It's as if people forget how to drive during the holidays. Can you imagine how much worse this would have been if it snowed on Saturn Island?"

Rick threw his head back, patting his ample stomach as he laughed.

The man had a point. A sprinkling of snow would cast this tiny island into utter panic. But they had enough drama without adding the weather to it.

"Where are you taking the van?" RJ asked the mechanic

Sunshine beamed her approval.

"Here." Rick plucked a business card from his top pocket and handed it to him.

RJ memorized the address and phone number before giving it to Sunshine.

They were on their way minutes after Sunshine arranged

for Rick to care for her vehicle.

They passed a few miles in silence, the engine's hum and the swish of the wheels their only accompaniment.

"So," Sunshine cleared her throat. "RJ, was it? How do you fit into the wedding? Are you Vivian's plus one?"

Maybe this wouldn't be so bad. He flashed a grin at Vivian. "Am I your plus one?"

"Did you ask me to be your date?" Vivian turned to Sunshine. "He's the twins' older brother."

"Oh, Robert Junior, got it. Thanks for picking me up. I can imagine your sisters panic at the thought of a missing groom's man and their wedding flowers."

RJ tightened his grip on the wheel. "That's why we didn't tell them."

"Hmm." Sunshine's disapproval thrummed in the silence.

"Look." Vivian drummed her fingers against the dashboard. "The twins have enough to worry about as they prepare for their big day.

"Not telling them was the best option in this situation." She squeezed his knee. "Besides, we have nothing to worry about. We'll get to the resort in plenty of time. But if you're a praying woman, start praying.

"In the meantime, we're listening to a contender for the title of Greatest Christmas Album of All Time." Vivian picked up his phone and hit play. Mariah Carey's rendition of Silent Night filled the air.

Sunshine burst into laughter. "I'm glad my husband Matt isn't here. This is not his favorite Christmas album."

Thirty

Chapter 30

Vivian exhaled a breath of relief as they drove through the resort gates. They had a little over an hour until the wedding.

RJ parked in front of the venue while she texted Robyn.

The wedding planner ran out to meet them. "Oh, thank God. I was worried you wouldn't make it on time. Sunshine, are you okay?"

"Yes," the florist responded. "I'm glad I followed my instinct and assembled everything beforehand."

Sunshine unloaded the bouquets. "Let's get these to the brides. RJ, my vote is with Mariah, but I hope you won't hold it against me and deliver the boutonnieres to the grooms and best men."

"You're mistaken, but I'll take care of it."

"Don't worry about the rest of the flowers." Vivian arched a brow at Robyn, who gave a tiny nod. "I'll deliver them to the right people."

No one would notice if she were late to the ceremony, but RJ would be missed. He reversed as she spoke, as if he too sensed the urgency.

"Hey," he said after parking in front of their villa. "I'm officially paired with Jacqui for the wedding, but I'll wish every moment that she was you."

Vivian's lips curved into a slow smile. "Don't let her hear you say that."

RJ gently caressed her face. "I want to kiss you so bad, but if I do, we'll be late for the wedding. Save me a dance, won't you?"

"I'll save all my dances for you." Not only tonight but for the rest of her life.

Her eyes locked with his. Could she already be falling in love?

How would she know if her feelings were real and not a result of being surrounded by weddings and couples in love?

"Vivian, I—"

A sharp rap on her window made her jerk, breaking their eye contact.

Her eyes widened as she spotted the woman standing beside the vehicle, designer heels tapping impatiently.

Vivian's fingers trembled as she lowered the window. "Mrs. Grant."

"If it's not too much trouble," the woman began in a frosty tone. "I'd like to get to my room and change."

"Of course not." She fumbled to unclasp her seatbelt. "No trouble at all."

RJ reached over to unlatch the belt. "Where's Mrs. Grant staying?" He brushed his thumb against the back of her hand, his touch centering her and reducing her anxiety.

"She's in the Nutcracker with us."

"What is this foolishness about nutcrackers?"

"Excellent." RJ's mouth curled into the parody of a smile. "Aren't we lucky?"

Vivian suppressed a snicker. "Stop it," she mumbled.

She did not want to get on Irene Grant's bad side. Not that Vivian had ever seen a good one. The woman was as standoffish as Vivian's parents. It was a miracle Cameron turned out as normal as he had.

RJ hopped out and rounded the car with a charming grin.

"Why don't I escort you ladies to your room?"

"I'm fine," she waved him off. A charming RJ and an uppity Irene Grant were too much for her to process. "I'll deliver the packages. Please show Mrs. Grant to her room."

Vivian did not want anyone, especially Irene, to learn how close they'd come to not having any flowers.

Thank You heavenly Father for working everything out.

Now if only He could slow time for them to get everything else in place.

* * *

Robyn fell into step with Vivian as she headed for the venue. The wedding planner had changed into a burgundy dress that complemented her curvy figure.

"We did it." Robyn touched Vivian's arm. "I couldn't have done it without you. Thanks for picking up Sunshine. I appreciate it."

"It's no trouble. I was glad to help."

The four-hour trip had cemented the bond between her and

RJ and made her crave more.

Did she and RJ have an actual shot at a relationship?

"So," Robyn drew the word out, "I feel like I should give you one of my cards."

"What?" She whipped her head to stare at Robyn.

The woman giggled, her expression mischievous. "I've seen the way he looks at you." Robyn bumped Vivian's shoulder. "And you can't tell me you're not interested. I've caught you checking him out on the sly."

"RJ and I are not…" she trailed off.

Why was her response always a denial that she had feelings for the man?

"May I give you some advice?" Robyn stopped walking, forcing Vivian to do the same.

She quirked a brow. "Do I have a choice?"

Robyn waited, patience emanating from her.

Vivian sighed. "Sure. What's your advice?"

"Don't push that man away. I know we're practically strangers, but after working on these weddings together and observing you this week, I feel I understand you."

Robyn took a deep breath as if what she had to say next would be hard, and Vivian braced herself.

"You strike me as a woman who is focused on her career. It's wonderful to be passionate about your job, but there will come a time when work is not fulfilling.

"God didn't create His children to be alone. RJ has powerful feelings for you, and maybe you wonder if a week is enough time to fall in love." Robyn shrugged. "Instead of stressing about how long you've known each other, focus on strengthening your bond.

"Don't let the man God created for you slip away because he

didn't follow your timeline. God's timing is perfect and we do better when we follow His rather than ours."

Robyn's words drifted through Vivian's mind long after the woman had left to perform her duties.

Vivian slid into a chair in the last row, golden sunlight warming her skin. Robyn and her team had done an excellent job transforming the hotel garden into the twins' dream wedding. Wooden chairs encircled the altar that was in the center.

They'd laid a white runner on the grass, an abundance of tropical blooms along the path on both sides.

Robyn had chosen orange, yellow, pink, and blue flowers that matched the twins' color scheme.

The brides and grooms were resplendent in their wedding finery, but Vivian only had eyes for RJ. He stood tall in his gray suit with an aquamarine shirt and rose-pink tie. His boutonniere included the colors of both brides. The perfect knight for a damsel in distress. For her.

"Do you, Cameron Grant, take Mackenzie Porter as your lawfully wedded wife?"

RJ's eyes met hers, and the intensity in his gaze made her breath catch.

"I do." RJ silently echoed the words, his gaze never leaving hers, and Vivian's heart melted into a puddle.

She was his. For better or for worse, in sickness and in health. She wanted to be with RJ more than she wanted to maintain the boundaries around her heart.

More than she wanted to prove that she wasn't her parents' daughter. She wanted...him.

"Me too," she whispered.

RJ's eyes darkened and she saw the herculean effort it took

for him to remain at the altar when he wanted to run to her.

Thirty-One

Chapter 31

W aiting was interminable. The longer RJ was away from Vivian, the harder it became to keep the smile on his face. As the photographer staged shot after shot, it became more of a grimace, maybe even a scowl.

He had never regretted agreeing to serve as groom's man to his sisters' spouses more than he did now. He wanted to be with Vivian. To find out if the two words she'd whispered meant the same to her as they did to him.

Jacqui leaned closer, per the photographer's request, and spoke through her fake smile. "Do you think we'll ever get out of here?"

RJ's smile became genuine. Good to know he wasn't the only one chafing to get to the reception.

"I'm pretty sure we'll be here for the rest of our lives."

The pretty woman snorted, earning a curious glance from Xavier and Madison.

He'd spent little time with the young woman who barely participated in the week's events, but he supposed he'd see her around. She was his niece's aunt, after all.

For now, he'd be a gentleman and help her through the torture they were forced to endure.

He spent the rest of the session distracting her, and himself, so they didn't lose their minds before the photographer released them.

She surprised him by having a snarky sense of humor. She'd make some man extremely lucky one day.

***

He and Jacqui sat at the head table beside each other, but like him, her attention was not on the proceedings. She scanned the room for the tenth time, searching for someone.

"Who are you looking for?"

"No one."

She dropped her gaze, her fingers twisting and untwisting the end of the white linen tablecloth.

A man on the outskirts of the dance floor caught RJ's eyes. He was of average height with broad shoulders and carried himself with an air of authority.

The man scanned their table, his eyes zeroing in on Jacqui. He headed for them, his expression resolute.

"Does your 'No One' look like that?" he directed Jacqui's attention to the man advancing on them.

Her head snapped up, such longing on her face that RJ became curious about their story. Apparently, he and Vivian weren't the only people who had a romance this week.

An usher intercepted the man before he disrupted Robyn's

carefully planned reception.

"Who is he?" RJ kept his voice low so as not to attract undue attention.

The soft murmur of laughter filled the air, punctuated by the clinking of glasses, while he waited for her response.

"Graham Isaacson—a man who is way out of my league."

"Graham Isaacson…why does that name seem familiar?"

She laughed, the sound so bitter that he stared at her with concern.

"Perhaps you are more in tune with the happenings of Saturn Island than I am."

"Hey, I don't know what happened between the two of you, but if you like each other…" he trailed off, searching for the words to encourage her to take a chance on love. "If you care for each other, don't let barriers keep you apart."

She snorted. "Even if he lied?"

He squirmed at the anger in her voice. "Lies are not always intended to hurt. Sometimes, they're meant to protect."

She turned the full force of her glare on him.

He raised both hands in defense. "I'm not saying it's okay. But try to see things from the other person's perspective before you decide what they did was unforgivable."

RJ was glad he'd accepted Elijah's job offer. How many half-truths and outright lies could he have told Vivian before he destroyed their relationship?

He whispered a quick prayer of thanksgiving that Vivian had forgiven him for his mistakes.

"It's time for the first dance of the evening," the deejay announced. "Mr. and Mrs. Cameron Grant, Mr. and Mrs. Xavier Washington, please take your spots on the dance floor." The deejay's excitement was palpable.

"I don't think you'll be able to avoid him much longer."

According to the program, the wedding party joined the couples and their parents for the third song.

"I know." Jacqui plopped her elbow on the table, her expression glum. "I wish I hadn't come to this stupid wedding."

He chuckled.

"Sorry." Jacqui stiffened. "I meant no disrespect to your sisters."

"It's fine." He squeezed Jacqui's shoulders, her despair motivating him to cheer her up.

Graham glowered at him, and RJ pulled back.

"Whatever lie Graham may have told you," RJ spoke through the side of his mouth, aware of Graham's glower aimed at him. "He cares about you."

RJ pulled Jacqui into his arms for the dance, holding her at a suitable distance. He didn't want Graham—or Vivian—to get any ideas something was going on.

Halfway through the song, the deejay invited the guests to join the wedding party on the dance floor.

"Get ready," he warned Jacqui as Graham headed for them.

She glanced over her shoulder, but Graham was beside RJ before she could rush off.

"May I cut in?"

The man's brusque tone was not asking for permission.

RJ relinquished Jacqui's hand. "Remember what I said." He nodded to Graham and left the floor, scanning the room for Vivian.

She hovered near a column, well away from the dancing couples. Time slowed as their eyes met across the room.

She was a vision in a royal blue ballgown that left her shoulders bare and a peek of one leg from the knee down.

His feet were in motion before he'd made a conscious decision to go to her.

"Hi." He gazed down at her, unable to form any more words.

"Hi." Her hands floated toward him and he held his breath as they settled on his shoulders.

"Would you like to dance?"

She beamed at him. "I thought you'd never ask."

He took her hand, guiding her past tables and guests, out of the ballroom. She laughed, her heels clicking along beside him.

"Where are we going?"

"Somewhere private."

"You're always stealing me away."

He glanced down at her. "That's because I want you all to myself."

He stopped at a room above the ballroom. He'd stumbled across it when he'd checked on the venues while filling in for Robyn. It was hidden from view, but the sounds of the reception drifted up to them.

The perfect setting to tell his woman he loved her—if he didn't chicken out.

Thirty-Two

Chapter 32

Vivian's heart sped up as RJ turned her to face him. The small room stood empty, its large window framing a breathtaking view of the night sky.

"Did you mean it?" His eyes were so intent on hers that it was hard to speak. "What am I saying?" He raked his hand over his head. "Of course you didn't mean it. You're not ready. What was I thinking?"

The man was unraveling before her. She'd done that. Her hesitancy and unwillingness to risk her heart had transformed the confident soldier into a bumbling mess. She rested a palm on his chest.

"Robert."

He stilled and she wasn't sure if it was because of her touch or her use of his given name.

"Yes?" He covered her hand with his.

"Are you planning to let me answer?"

He drew in a breath. "Go ahead."

Vivian closed her eyes, reliving the moment she realized she was all in for this relationship.

She was worthy of love. She was capable of love. Not because of who her parents were, but because of who God is.

"I'm not ready to get married." She would pray for God to give her victory over her fears in that area, too. "But," she wet her lips.

"But...?" RJ stepped closer, his chest pressing against her palm.

"I'm ready to be in a committed relationship with the right man." She flexed her fingers until his hold loosened. "A relationship I hope will eventually lead to marriage. I know the perfect wedding planner."

Robyn's advice had helped Vivian consider what RJ meant to her.

"Do you have someone in mind for your groom?" His gravelly voice sent shivers down her spine.

"Uh-huh." She walked her fingers up his chest.

"Don't keep me in suspense." RJ skimmed the curve of her ear. "Tell me who this man is. I need to know if I should have a serious talk with him."

"He's strong, loyal, fiercely protective of those he cares about."

She replayed the multiple times RJ had protected her from a physical or emotional threat.

"He's also sweet, loves Christmas with all its traditions," she wound her arms around his neck. "He has dubious taste in music, but I'll forgive him because I'm worse."

She giggled at his wounded expression.

"Your guy sounds like a wuss." RJ led her into a waltz, moving her effortlessly across the floor.

Why was she surprised this man was an excellent dancer?

"He excels at everything he does."

"Everything?" RJ's warm breath tickled her ear.

"I'm not sure about his kisses, though. He might need more practice."

He growled, pulling her fully against him. "I'm a fantastic kisser."

"Prove it." She tugged his head down to hers. "Shut up and kiss me, Soldier Boy."

"I thought you'd never ask, My Queen of Curves."

Stars exploded behind her eyes when their lips met and it took a second for Vivian to realize it was a firework display.

RJ tightened his grip on her, intensifying the kiss until she felt as if she were floating.

Her entire life, she'd wanted to matter to someone. RJ's kiss told her she'd finally met that person. She surrendered her heart, trusting him to keep it safe.

* * *

Instead of returning to the reception, they headed to the villa, where RJ changed into sweatpants and a t-shirt, and she exchanged her gown for a short jumper.

"What exactly are we doing?"

Craft items encircled them on the living room floor, the twinkle of the Christmas tree lights casting a festive glow.

"We're finishing the gifts." He scanned the list in the Nutcracker group chat. "We're almost done, but there are a few left."

"Alright." She made a show of cracking her fingers. "I'm

yours to instruct, Soldier Boy."

"Are you?" He tugged her onto his lap, his eyes lingering on her lips.

"Yes." Her words came out breathy.

"Prove it," he whispered against her mouth before covering it with his.

Vivian lost track of the time as RJ used his lips to convince her of his complete adoration.

He hadn't said it, but she wondered if he loved her. Perhaps eventually he'd give her the words she hadn't realized she needed.

"You are a distraction." RJ scooted back, his chest heaving. "Stay." He put more distance between them. "Give me a minute."

He took several deep breaths to get himself under control while Vivian bit back a grin and tried not to kiss him again.

He was doing a fabulous job of convincing her she was desirable. With RJ, she'd never be at the bottom of his list.

Thanks for allowing RJ's path to cross mine, Lord.

"Okay." He met her gaze, a smile teasing the corner of his lips. "I don't get to kiss you until we complete our tasks."

"Then I suggest we start because I didn't agree to that plan and I'm not sure how long I can survive without another kiss."

His nostrils flared, but he remained on his side. Pity.

He pulled up an image of a craft on his phone. "This is what we're making for Diane and Carl. It's simple. All you have to do is…"

He demonstrated the technique to make a picture frame using fudge sticks. She mimicked him, surprised at how easy it was to follow his instructions.

"I never considered myself crafty, but this is fun."

He grinned. "You can learn anything from the right teacher. I look forward to learning from and teaching you new things, Vee."

"Me too."

She was a bit fearful of her and RJ becoming hyper-focused on each other. But she'd seen enough healthy relationships up close this week that her fear lessened daily.

Thirty-Three

Chapter 33

A bell clanged outside Vivian's door, startling her awake. She bolted upright.

"What on earth?"

She jerked the door open to stare into RJ's beaming face. "Merry Christmas."

She covered the lower half of her face, not wanting to kill him with her morning breath.

"Merry Christmas. What are you doing?"

He wagged his brows. "This is a Porter family tradition, and for better or worse, you're one of us now."

The tingles started in her toes until they spread throughout her entire body.

"You realize I'm not the one who got married yesterday, right?"

His eyes darkened. "You made a commitment to me and I'm holding you to it." His gaze roamed over her from head to toe.

"Brush your teeth, QC. I'll be back in two minutes for my good morning kiss."

"Suppose I don't want to?" She popped a hip, feigning reluctance.

"I have no problem kissing you now." He reached for her, his intention clear.

Vivian did the first thing that came to mind and slammed the door in his face.

"Sorry."

He chuckled. "Two minutes." He lowered his voice. "I'll be back for my kiss."

The bells jingled, waking the rest of the household. She suspected someone was in the other villas doing the same thing. Since the twins had moved in with their spouses, they were probably on wake-up duty.

She sprinted to the bathroom, brushing her teeth and washing her face in record time. The crown braids from the wedding remained intact, but she wet her fingers and re-twisted the tendrils that had unraveled around her face.

There were two sharp raps at the door. She drew it open, and before she could say a word, RJ had backed her against it and slanted his mouth over hers.

As it did every time their lips met, sensation washed over her. She gripped his shoulders and held on, kissing him as thoroughly as he kissed her.

"Are congratulations in order?" Margaret's teasing comment jolted them apart.

"I'm not attending another wedding for at least twelve months," Bob grumbled.

Vivian hid her face against RJ's neck.

"Go away, Mom and Dad. You'll scare her."

"You're lucky it wasn't one of your sisters or Avery." Margaret's voice faded as she moved further down the corridor.

"Where were we?" RJ nuzzled her shoulder, recapturing her attention.

"She's right." Vivian pushed against his chest until he moved. "Can you imagine what would happen if Avery caught us?"

She mock-shuddered. They'd learned early that Avery had a knack for making up parodies, and no one was safe from her impromptu songs.

"Fine."

He leaned against the doorjamb. "I wanted to give you a gift before we went downstairs."

Uncertainty streaked across his face, and she frowned in concern.

"What is it?"

"It's not much, just a token to remember our time here."

She spread both hands. "Gimme."

She hadn't received many gifts in her lifetime, which made every item more precious.

RJ bent to pick up a box and handed it to her. It was heavier than she'd expected from the small size.

"Do you want to…?" She left the question hanging, entered her room, and sat at the small table.

She peeled off the wrapping paper to reveal an intricately carved tree house with a couple standing on the tiny steps, their detailed faces almost lifelike.

She gasped. "This is exquisite." Her eyes darted to his. "Thank you, but I thought this was a no-spend gift exchange?"

He shuffled his weight from one foot to the next. "I didn't buy it."

She frowned at him. "What do you mean?"

His lips twisted into an amused smile. "Look closely at the couple, QC."

Her frown deepened, but she did as he asked. "Is this—" She blinked, unable to believe her eyes. "They resemble us."

Vivian's eyes darted between RJ and the carving.

"Yeah." RJ ran a hand over his head. "That's because they are."

Her mind whirred as she put the pieces together. Vivian's fingers brushed over the smooth wood, tracing the ridges of the detailed carving.

"You made this."

He shrugged.

"RJ," she swallowed hard as possibilities flooded her mind. "Why aren't you making carvings for your family's store?"

"Because the family business is focused on antiques, not modern statues?" His shoulders bunched around his ears. "No one would buy them."

"You're wrong. People would pay to have your carvings in their homes. They'd pay even more for custom designs. How did you do this?"

When? She couldn't imagine the number of hours he spent carving such an intricate piece.

"I used the photo I took of us as a model. But, Viv, come on, it's a block of wood. No one's going to pay me for that."

"You're wrong, and I'll prove it to you." Her fingers closed around the statue.

"What are you doing?" He came toward her but she sidestepped him.

"Proving you wrong." She strode from the room with RJ on her heels.

He could have overtaken her, but she suspected a part of him craved validation as much as the next person. And she was glad, because there was no way she could have outpaced him to the living where the families had gathered if he hadn't.

"What do you think of this?" Vivian thrust the carving under Bob's nose.

The man perched his glasses on his nose and examined it. "It's well done. This level of craftsmanship in modern designs is rare. Where did you get it?"

Vivian ignored his question. "Would you sell this in your shop?"

"Let me see." The twins spoke simultaneously as they rushed to their father's side, one peering over each shoulder.

"Oh, these would sell like hot bread." Mackenzie ran a finger over the statue. "If we set up a display near the front, they'd attract people into the store."

"This almost looks…" Madison's gaze moved between Vivian and the carving.

"Yes?" Vivian prompted.

"It makes no sense." Madison tilted her head. "You'll think I'm crazy."

Mackenzie bumped her twin's shoulder. "We already know you're crazy. You may as well say it."

The others gathered behind the Porters, passing the carving from one person to the next.

"It resembles Vivian and RJ!" Cynthia's comment elicited gasps.

"It does," agreed Diane. "How is that possible?"

"Because…" Vivian waited until everyone's attention was on her. "RJ made it."

Chapter 34

No one spoke for several moments after Vivian's revelation. RJ braced himself for his father's censure.

"Son?" Bob spoke first. "Is this true?"

"Yes, Dad."

"Explain yourself." Bob's scowl was fierce.

Despite the discipline he gained from countless missions, his father had a knack for loosening his tongue.

"Intelligence work can be boring. I taught myself how to whittle using YouTube videos and online tutorials. I practiced every chance I had until I got better."

He inhaled deeply, the comforting scents of cinnamon and pine filling his lungs as he tried to steady his nerves.

Bob stroked his chin. "I see. You told me you didn't want to inherit the legacy that my grandfather started."

RJ stiffened. "Dad, I—"

Bob raised a hand, cutting off RJ's rebuttal.

"I don't plan to rehash the old argument."

The tightness between RJ's shoulder blades eased.

"Madison and I are passionate about preserving the past. We like restoring old things. It's in our blood."

The old shame crept up RJ's neck, the hot, prickling wave, causing the blood to roar in his ears until his father's words became a muffled hum.

Vivian crossed the room, wrapping an arm around his waist. He embraced her, her soft curves pulling him out of the past and anchoring him in the present.

"You and Mackenzie," Bob continued, "are more like Granddad than I am."

"Come again?" RJ gaped, sure he hadn't heard right.

"Are you feeling okay, Dad?" Mackenzie gawked at their father with an equally gobsmacked expression.

"Did I stutter?" Bob glared at them. "We excel at restoring old things." Bob gestured to himself and Madison. "But you," he jabbed his fingers at RJ and Mackenzie, "are innovating ways for us to stay relevant for the next generation."

RJ blinked. His father had drummed it into their heads that they wouldn't change anything.

"I thought, 'If it was good enough for your grandfather, it's good enough for us'?"

His sisters joined him on the refrain.

Bob narrowed his eyes. "Didn't realize I'd raised comedians. How long does it take you to complete a carving?"

RJ shrugged. "A few days or weeks. It depends on what I have going on and how complex the design is."

Bob cleared his throat. "Forever Furnished will be happy to sell any carvings you want to offload."

"We'd like exclusive rights." Mackenzie chimed in.

"You'll need a name for your product line." Xavier rubbed his hands. "I'm exceptional at making up things."

"I want to place an order for my wife's birthday in February." Carl Washington squeezed his wife's shoulder.

RJ's temples throbbed as the stream of orders overwhelmed him. He massaged his forehead. This was far from what he'd expected.

Vivian beamed. "I told you."

"So you did." RJ wrapped his arms around her.

"Uncle RJ," Gracie tugged on his t-shirt. "Do you think we can open our presents now?"

He chuckled, running his hand over the girl's twists. "I can arrange that."

He put two fingers in his mouth and blew a shrill whistle. Everyone stared at him.

"We're boring the kids. Can we get to the presents now?"

"Mine." Jadon shrieked, reaching for the carving.

"Oh, no, sweet boy," Vivian weaved through the crowd and grabbed the carving before Jadon's fingers closed around it. "This belongs to Auntie Viv. But you can play with it if you let me hold you." She wriggled the carving.

"Yours?" Jadon scrunched up his face as if the concept of something not belonging to him was foreign.

"Yes." Vivian opened her arms. "Will you come to Aunt Viv?"

"Okay." Jadon stretched from his father's arms to Vivian's.

She held him awkwardly at first, but after a few tips from Ella and Conner, she adjusted and cradled the toddler like a pro.

Everything clicked into place for RJ. He didn't know when, where, or how, but he would marry Vivian and they'd make beautiful babies.

"I see you took our advice." Xavier crept up to RJ's left.

"I'm taking all the credit," Cameron said from his right. "Did you enjoy your couple's massage?"

RJ cut his gaze between the two men. "You'll do."

Xavier frowned. "What's that supposed to mean?"

"I always wanted brothers," RJ responded. "Madison and Mackenzie could have made worse choices." His brothers-in-law were men he admired. "But if you hurt my sisters, I will search for you," he clapped a hand on their shoulders, "and I will find you."

Thirty-Five

Chapter 35

She didn't know why she'd reached for Jadon. She'd avoided him, Avery, and Gracie for the entire week, as she wasn't sure how to relate to children.

At first, she clutched the toddler, fearful of dropping him. After a few minutes, she relaxed her hold and savored his sweet baby powder scent.

She had a lot to learn before she was ready to care for a child, but for the first time, she believed she could.

She slanted a glance at RJ. Did he want children? He was wonderful with them.

Gracie and Avery hadn't left his side since he'd redirected the families to the Christmas gift exchange. Everyone had gathered around the tree. The older adults sat on the couches and chairs while the rest were on the floor.

The girls handed RJ the parcels and he read the names before passing the gift to its rightful owner.

"Jadon." RJ handed off a cylindrical package.

"This is yours." Vivian gave the boy the package.

"Here." Ella was beside her in an instant. "Let me help."

She gladly handed over the boy. She'd hold him later.

"Vivian."

She accepted a large square package, angling it so the Christmas tree lights danced across the colorful paper.

Avery bounced. "I helped with that."

She tentatively unwrapped the gift while trying to figure out what it was. She and RJ had bought lots of stuff, but nothing this large.

"It's an organizer." Vivian touched the brightly wrapped pen holder.

Anna smiled at her. "We figured you'd appreciate it since you were Cameron's assistant."

"I do." She'd keep it on her desk to remind her that families came in all shapes and sizes. "Thank you."

"We used cereal boxes," Avery giggled, "and toilet paper rolls."

Levi rolled his eyes. "You're not supposed to tell her, squirt."

"It's okay." Vivian grinned at the girl. "I'll save my cereal boxes and tubes for when I need a replacement."

Vivian smiled as she watched the others, their faces alight with joy and contentment, as they unwrapped their handmade gifts. This was the true spirit of Christmas.

It wasn't about who spent the most money or bought the fanciest gift. It was about sharing an experience they'd remember for years to come.

* * *

RJ tucked her arm in his as they exited the small chapel after the Christmas Day service. The couples had gifted them an additional day at the resort, and she was savoring every moment.

"What did you enjoy most about today?"

"Hmm." Vivian pondered his question.

They'd done many wonderful things that day, and it was only 10 a.m.

"The service. I love the reminder that Christ gave up the luxuries of heaven to experience hardship so He could better understand the human experience."

"I always think about that." RJ drew her along a path toward the resort's exit. "Few kings would give up their kingdom to be mistreated by their subjects."

"It's especially poignant when you remember the King is omnipotent, omniscient, and omnipresent."

"There are many things Christ could have done instead of dying for humanity."

"Yes." Gratitude for the Savior's gift filled her heart. "We are truly blessed."

"We are." RJ stopped at the gate and turned to cradle her face. "I am extremely grateful that God brought us together. You are a precious gift, and I want to treasure you for the rest of my life."

"RJ." Her heart sped up when he stared at her—as if she were the most beautiful woman in the entire world.

"Vivian," he mimicked her inflection. "I have another gift for you. This one wasn't free, but I thought you'd enjoy it."

"You're spoiling me."

"It's a privilege to care for you. Close your eyes."

She did and then popped one eye open to peek at him.

He laughed. "I knew you'd do that."

"You did not." She shoved him playfully.

"I did." He pulled a purple scarf from his pocket. "That's why I borrowed this." He quickly tied the scarf around her eyes.

"I'll fall and break my ankles," she mock-grumbled.

"I can always carry you." His voice rumbled near her ear.

"You can't. I'm too heavy."

RJ swept her into his arms, and her breath caught in surprise. She shrieked, clutching his shoulders.

"Put me down! You'll drop me."

She could hardly breathe, expecting him to buckle under her weight any second.

"My backpack is heavier than you."

Oh, my.

She snuggled her face against his neck, relishing his spicy cologne as he carried her.

The walk was over much too soon.

"I'm putting you down." He lowered her to the ground, keeping his arm around her as the world settled into place. "And removing the scarf."

He did and Vivian blinked a few times at the image before her, certain it was a mirage.

"A carriage?"

A white horse and a covered carriage, complete with a driver in a top hat, waited for them.

"After you, My Curvy Queen," RJ swept into a bow before helping her onto the cushioned seat.

Vivian sank into the plush seat, the cool morning air brushing her cheeks as the rhythmic clip-clop of the horse's hooves filled the air.

She kissed him on the cheek. "Thank you."

The man was going all out to win her heart when it wasn't

necessary. She was already his—all she needed was the courage to tell him.

Thirty-Six

Chapter 36

RJ didn't consider himself a romantic person. He saw a problem, analyzed it, found a solution, and executed the plan. But Vivian made him want to quote poetry and serenade her—even though he was a terrible singer.

She tucked her arm through his and rested her head on his shoulder. Her heady fragrance drove him crazy, activating the ticking clock in his mind. Their time was running out, and he hadn't told her the most important thing.

He jiggled his knee as he contemplated the best way to tell her how he felt.

"Okay," Vivian pulled away. "What's wrong? You rented a beautiful carriage to take us on a scenic trip around Greenvale, and I doubt you've seen a single thing."

RJ stared into her beloved face. "You're right. I'm distracted." He skimmed his fingers along her jawline. "I need to tell you something."

Apprehension skipped across her face, her eyes becoming wary. "Go ahead."

He swallowed hard, his mind racing as he silently prayed for courage. "We haven't known each other long, but I want to spend the rest of my life with you, Vivian. I want you to meet me at the altar where we'll exchange vows until death parts us."

He lay a hand against her stomach. "I want to start a family with you, watching your body blossom with our child."

Her eyes filled with tears.

"I want—" Everything. He shook his head. "I'm doing a terrible job."

"No," her voice was shaky. "You're doing an excellent job." She covered his hand with hers. "I want..." she trailed off, her tongue darting out to moisten her lips. "I want those things too."

RJ drew closer to her on the narrow bench, grateful for the carriage's covering. "There's one other thing I want more than anything."

He ran his eyes over her face, allowing an inkling of his love for her to shine through.

"Oh?" She raised a shaky hand to cup his cheek. "The Bible says to ask for what you want."

He took a deep breath. *Please, God.* "Your heart. I love you, Vivian. I am in love with you, and I've been driving myself crazy thinking I'll scare you away by telling you before you're ready."

"Shh." She pressed a finger against his lips. "I'm not sure what romantic love feels like, but if it's a constant sensation that butterflies have invaded my stomach..."

"Or a fullness in my chest because I'm so happy and want to

burst into song like I'm in a musical." She gave him a soft smile that lit up her face. "If it's wanting to spend every moment with the person who elicits those feelings," she caressed his face, her touch warm and soft. "Then I'm in love with you."

He crushed his lips to hers, unable to wait another moment. She loved him with the same depth of emotion that he felt for her.

He cradled her head, angling her face to deepen their kiss. She loved him. The road ahead wouldn't be smooth as they navigated their lives together, but he was prepared to do the hard work to nurture their relationship. He prayed she would, too.

"Ahem."

The abrupt throat clearing brought him out of the haze their kiss had created.

"Sorry to disturb you, Sir, Miss." The carriage driver began in an amused tone. "I'd love to give you the time to…finalize things, but I have another ride booked in a few minutes."

"What?"

"We're here." The old man gestured to the imposing wall.

"Oh." RJ blinked several times before he registered they were back at the resort. "Oh." He hopped out of the carriage and helped Vivian down. "Sorry about that." He gave the man a generous tip.

"No worries." The driver chuckled. "The number of love confessions this carriage has witnessed would surprise you." He winked. "Especially at this time of the year.

"Congratulations. I pray the Lord will bless your union and you'll be together for many happy years."

The man tipped his hat and jiggled the harness until the horse plodded away.

"Well," Vivian stared after him, a huge grin on her face. "That's the first time I've ever taken a romantic carriage ride, only to miss the whole thing."

He wrapped his arms around her, pulling her into his chest. "We can do it again sometime."

"Nah." She turned, wrapping her arms around his neck. "I'd much rather kiss the man I love."

"Happy to oblige." He lowered his head and picked up where they'd left off.

* * *

RJ and Vivian lingered in the living room of the Nutcracker Palace.

His sisters and their husbands had left early for their honeymoon. The others waited outside for the luxury bus Cameron had hired to take them home.

He would miss this place—not the building, its atmosphere. A week ago, he came to the villa broken, angry, and lost. He had no direction and was on the verge of changing careers.

Now he had two exciting opportunities. One allowed him to use the skills he'd acquired in the last sixteen years and the other contributed to his family's legacy.

Vivian trailed a finger over the couch. "I'll miss this place."

"Me too." He slung an arm around her shoulder.

"When will I see you again?" She avoided looking at him.

"Hey," he faced her. "Didn't I tell you I was moving to Portsville?"

"Yes, but—" she shrugged. "Your job doesn't start until after the new year. You'll need to pack up your stuff in Cinnamon Hill and move across the country. It'll be weeks before I see you again."

He chuckled. "You underestimate your appeal and my determination to be with you. Elijah has an apartment ready for me to move in.

"I'll leave for a few days to finish my contract. But it's official. I'm moving to Portsville." He showed her a key. "I rented an SUV. I'll drive you home if you don't mind stopping in Cinnamon Hill to pick up my clothes."

A slow smile crept over her face. "I suppose you have another playlist of hit songs I must listen to."

He grinned. "You know it."

"Well," she walked her fingers up his arm. "My boss gave me two weeks off. I could spend them showing you around the city."

"I accept your invitation." He placed his hands on her hips and tugged her closer. "There's one thing I need your help with."

"Anything."

"I need to stock up on fuel," he murmured against her lips, "it's a long drive."

"Happy to oblige." She captured his lips and RJ sank into the kiss.

God's ability to redeem and restore amazed him. He couldn't wait for the adventures he and Vivian would have as they followed the path God laid out for them.

Epilogue

Jacqui sat at the back of the bus, away from the chatter of her parents and everyone returning to their homes.

She'd had wonderful experiences this week. But her heartbreak was at the forefront of her thoughts as she stared at the villa Gracie had dubbed Nutcracker Palace.

Gray—no, Graham's—face came unbidden to her thoughts, eliciting a bittersweet smile. She believed she had finally met a man who saw past her facade to her true self.

She snorted, earning a curious look from Ella. The woman stared at her, a wealth of compassion in her eyes—as if she understood what Jacqui was going through. But how could she?

The only person who knew what happened this week was RJ, and he wasn't the sort to betray someone's trust. She'd given him an earful about lying men at the reception.

Besides, he and Vivian were still inside. Jacqui was glad RJ got his happy ending because she sure wouldn't. A tear crept down her cheek, and she used a finger to wipe it away.

The worst thing about Gray's deception was that he hadn't only hurt her. He'd hurt Samelia. The thought of the tween dredged up another bitter smile.

After a rocky start, Jacqui had bonded with the girl. When her relationship with Gray turned romantic, she'd hoped she and Samelia would get what they wanted—a family of their own.

A flash of blue beside the villa attracted her attention. A child peeked around the corner.

Jacqui grasped the armrest as the bus lurched, its engine rumbling. As the bus moved, Samelia's head snapped up. The girl's eyes darted over the windows, scanning each one intently as if searching for someone.

Searching for her.

She pressed her palm against the cool glass, the smooth surface offering no comfort for the emptiness inside. Samelia lifted her hand in a forlorn wave.

The bus pulled away from the curb, forcing Jacqui to face the inevitable. She was returning to Idlewood even more bereft than she'd left. From the corner of her eyes, she glimpsed the man standing behind Samelia, his hand on her shoulder.

Graham.

For a moment, she'd dreamed of love and family. But Graham's lies had proven how unrealistic such dreams were for a woman like her.

She'd built up her hopes only for them to crumble like sand beneath her fingertips. The trouble with sand scattered by the wind was you could never recapture all the grains.

* * *

Jacqui believes her dreams of love and family are hopeless because Graham lied to her. Can she forgive Graham? Or is this separation the end of their journey? Find out in A Daughter for Christmas.

***

RJ is keeping a secret from Vivian. Will it create tension in their relationship? Or will it be the answer to Vivian's prayers?

Join my newsletter community and read the bonus scene for free: https://bookhip.com/GLWDQRD.

Author's Note

Thanks for reading RJ and Vivian's story. Both characters struggled with the weight of parental expectations.

RJ's father wanted him to take a role in the family business, regardless of his wishes. Robert Senior was more concerned about passing on his family's legacy than what RJ wanted.

Vivian grew up with neglectful parents who taught her love had to be earned. Despite her efforts to be perfect, she never earned her parents' approval or acceptance.

This left her with the false belief that she needed to attain perfection to be accepted.

Maybe you've also struggled with parental expectations. In most cases, parents are not trying to harm their children by holding them to a certain standard.

Rather, they're trying to teach their children the importance of working toward a goal.

Parents are not the only people who put expectations on us. Our employers, spouses, friends, and the state expect certain behaviors from us. God also expects His children to behave in a particular manner.

So how should you respond when someone's expectations

clash with your desires or dreams?

Let me first state: some expectations cannot be escaped.

A country has laws that its citizens must obey.

Your parents, teachers, and superiors expect obedience and deserve respect.

Spouses, children, and other family members have needs that must be met.

The key to navigating unrealistic expectations is to align yourself with God.

What does your heavenly Father expect from you?

For example, if someone asks you to do something that requires you to disregard God's Law, your option is to please God rather than man.

If God has placed a dream in your heart and someone wants you to go in the opposite direction, you must obey God.

If God expects you to perform a task, focus on doing that. Will it be easy?

No. The moment you decide to obey God's plan for your life, the enemy sets out to oppose you.

He will turn family and friends against you. He'll put obstacles in your path. Satan will use every resource in his immense artillery to prevent you from meeting God's expectations.

But God has not left you alone to follow His instructions. He has given you the Holy Spirit, who strengthens you. He has given you the Holy Scriptures to guide you.

The weapons God has equipped us with are powerful. They can tear down strongholds and allow us to stand against the evil one.

Are you struggling with the pang of unrealistic expectations?

Spend time in prayer, asking God to reveal His will for you.

Ask Him for the words to speak to those who put this unwanted pressure on you (if you discern that it's His will for you to confront the person).

Let the person know that their desires for you go against your wishes or God's plans for your life.

My friend, I pray that you'll be freed from unrealistic expectations, and will turn to God and allow Him to work out His plans for your life.

About Aminata

Aminata Coote's passionate love affair with books began with an upside-down copy of Silas Marner. She writes stories that aim to point to a God bigger than our failings and provide hope to others.

Aminata lives in Montego Bay, Jamaica with her husband and son. She is the author of several Bible studies and devotionals, including *God Is In Control: 21 Devotions About the Sovereignty of God.*

Connect with her on her website, aminatacoote.com. Follow her on Instagram or Facebook @aminatacoote.

Sign up for Aminata's newsletter at https://bookhip.com/GLWDQRD and read the bonus scene for free.

Other Books by Aminata

Inspirational Contemporary Romance

Orange Valley Series
His Perfect Wife
His Perfect Match
His Perfect Family
His Perfect Choice

Christmas with the Porters
A Husband for Christmas
A Family for Christmas
A Wife For Christmas
A Daughter for Christmas

The Firefighters of Orange Valley
Falling For Her Fake Wedding Date
Falling For Her Student's Single Dad
Falling For Her Grumpy Neighbor

Sweet Haven

A Wife For Christmas

Her Rock Star Husband
The Mother of His Child
Her Best Friend's Secret

Christmas in Orange Valley
The Doctor's Christmas Miracle

Hearts Unveiled
Finding Peace in Orange Valley
Finding Love in Orange Valley
Finding Joy in Orange Valley

Orange Valley Shorts
How It Began: His Perfect Wife Prequel
I'll Wait For You: His Perfect Family Prequel

Devotionals
How To Find Your Gratitude Attitude
Draw Closer 52-Week Devotional Journal
Praying Your Way Through Social Media: Reflections for
Christian Artists and Entrepreneurs (collaboration with
Latasha Strachan)
God Sees You: 21 Devotions for the Woman Who Feels
Invisible
The Battle Is Not Yours: 21 Devotions for Spiritual Warfare
God Is In Control: 21 Devotions on God's Sovereignty

Learn more about my books at
https://tinyurl.com/ACooteBooks